THE FELLOWSHIP OF THE HAND

THE FELLOWSHIP

Books by Edward D. Hoch

THE SHATTERED RAVEN
THE JUDGES OF HADES
THE TRANSVECTION MACHINE
THE SPY AND THE THIEF
CITY OF BRASS
DEAR DEAD DAYS (editor)
THE FELLOWSHIP OF THE HAND

OF THE HAND

BY
EDWARD
D. HOCH

 WALKER AND COMPANY ▪ New York

First published in the United States of America in 1973
by the Walker Publishing Company, Inc.

Published simultaneously in Canada by Fitzhenry &
Whiteside, Limited, Toronto.

ISBN: 0-8027-5553-4

Library of Congress Catalog Card Number: 72-83115

Printed in the United States of America.

10 9 8 7 6 5 4 3 2 1

For
HANS STEFAN SANTESSON
who started it all.

1.
EARL JAZINE

The circuits spun off in a dozen directions from the core unit, reminding Earl Jazine of an intricately filigreed spider's web caught in the early morning sunshine. At another time he might have thought the sight pretty, but cramped as he was within the bowels of the FRIDAY-404 election computer there was little space or time for such aesthetic delights.

"All right," he said into his wrist intercom, "start the power."

There was a gentle hum in the wires about him, and his induction meters told him that all power was flowing smoothly. The core unit brightened and began to transmit. Jazine waited another five minutes and then squeezed backwards out of the machine.

"Find anything?" Rogers asked.

"Just that I need to lose weight if I'm going to stay in this line of work." Jazine wiped the sweat from his hands. "The unit seems to be functioning perfectly. What you've got is a job for an electronics technician, not the Computer Cops." He almost winced when he said the name, knowing how his boss Carl Crader hated it. But that was what the newsmen had dubbed the bureau, for better or worse, and Jazine

1

admitted he found it a handy tag when describing his job.

"You don't seem to understand the problem," Harry Rogers said. He was young, just out of space college, and with all the assurance of youth. Jazine, at thirty-one, felt like an old man next to his boyish freshness.

"Is that so? Suppose you tell me again."

"Well, sir, I was running a check on this unit for the November election and I ran into some pre-programming. That's illegal, of course, so I reported it immediately to Washington. I guess they figured it was a job for the Computer Cops."

"Sure," Jazine agreed. Whenever somebody tampered with a stock market computer, or programmed surgery, or just the computerized parking meter at the jetport, it was a job for the Computer Cops. He was used to it by now, and sometimes the assignments were even interesting. This wasn't one of the times. "Well, I'll climb back inside and you do a read-out. I'll see if we're getting any feed off another system."

"How could we get feed off another system?" the young man argued. "This is a closed circuit, regulated by the election laws!"

"Well, let's just see now."

There were certain advantages to computerized election returns, not the least of which was that the irregular vote-counting methods of the twentieth century were completely eliminated. Every voting machine in the United States of America and Canada was tied into the system, which enabled Washington and every home in the USAC to watch the actual

2

tabulation as each vote was cast. There was a central FRIDAY-404 computer serving every 10,000 individual voting machines, and as the data came into it by microwave relay it was coded and transmitted to the skysphere satellite and then on to Washington. There television and teleprinters took over the task of transmitting the running totals into every American home.

The first presidential election to be fully computerized, back in 2032, had caused an uproar by showing Thurgood leading Stokes through most of the balloting. Then, as the votes from the West Coast and the ocean states drifted in, the tide suddenly turned. The next day Thurgood supporters were blaming their man's defeat on the computerized results—claiming overconfident Thurgood supporters stayed home late in the day, while the trailing Stokes mustered his western people to win a victory in the final minutes of polling there.

But such a thing had never happened again, and the seesawing election battles of recent years had become more exciting than an antelope race. The incumbent, President McCurdy, had won reelection in a contest that saw the lead change twenty-two times in the course of the day. No one could complain that the new system failed to bring out the vote. Fully ten million more citizens were casting their ballots these days.

Of course the system meant one more job for the Computer Cops, who inherited the policing of elections from the Justice Department. An independent department situated in New York and reporting directly to the President, the Computer Investigation Bureau was responsible for the fairness of elections

3

and the accuracy of the FRIDAY-404 system. With any voting machine, the easiest method of falsifying the returns was to cast a number of fraudulent ballots in advance, registering them on the machine before the actual vote began. Theoretically, the same thing could be done with the FRIDAY-404 through pre-programming, which was why young Rogers had been checking it out five weeks before the election. What he'd found had brought Earl Jazine to the scene.

"Power on," Jazine said into his wrist intercom. "One more time." He watched the central core for a moment and then said, "Now do a printout."

When the computer had shut itself off automatically, he squeezed himself out again and took the sheet of printout symbols from the teleprinter.

OOOOOOOOOOOOOOOOOOOOOOOOOOO
XXXXXXXXXXXXXXXXXXXXXXXXXX
JASONBLUNTOOOOOOO364550OOOO
STANLEYAMBROSEOOO453900OOOO
XXXXXXXXXXXXXXXXXXXXXXXXXX

Jazine frowned at the sheet of paper. "Give me a clear," he said.

Rogers pressed another button and the teleprinter chattered some brief symbols.

JASON BLUNT 36455
STANLEY AMBROSE 45390

"Who the hell are Blunt and Ambrose?"

"It seems to be the results of some election. Maybe a local one from last year."

Jazine shook his head. "The figures couldn't stay in the machine this long, not after it was cleared."

"So who would feed them in now, a month before

4

election? And with those names! Who are they?"

"Neither one is running for president, I can tell you that," Jazine said. "Let me take this back to New York and see what the boss thinks."

"You agree with me finally that something's wrong here?"

Jazine studied the printout again. "I agree that something's not right. That's about as much commitment as you'll get out of me for now."

The Computer Investigation Bureau was located on the top floor of the World Trade Center in lower Manhattan. Taken over by the federal government some fifty years earlier, the twin-towered giant had long since ceased to be the world's tallest building— an honor it had held, actually, for only a few seasons. But for CIB purposes it was still the perfect headquarters, centrally located in the heart of the computerized business community, and with a flat roof for quick rocketcopter flights anywhere in the country. Best of all, it was far enough from the bureaucratic jungle of Washington to maintain some sort of independence.

Earl Jazine waved to Judy, Carl Crader's tall blond secretary, as he hurried through the air door into the director's private office. Crader was thirty years older than Earl, with streaks of gray hair and a developing paunch that he tried to hide. In many ways he was the most powerful and respected head of a government bureau in a hundred years—since the peak of J. Edgar Hoover's popularity.

"Back so soon?" he greeted Jazine, glancing up from his perennially cluttered desk. "Anything doing on that trouble report?"

"Something doing, all right, chief, but I don't know what." He produced the printout from the election computer and passed it across the desk.

Carl Crader glanced at the names and numbers. "Who are Blunt and Ambrose?"

"That's what I'd like to know. Their names are pre-programmed into that FRIDAY-404 unit. It was causing the trouble Rogers reported."

Crader frowned and scratched his head. "Any ideas?"

"I already checked last year's campaigns in every state. No one named Blunt or Ambrose ran for anything. There's a Stanley Ambrose who used to be head of the Venus Colony, but he's not in politics."

"Where does that leave us?" Crader asked. He was always anxious to collect his subordinates' opinions before committing his own thoughts on a subject.

Jazine hesitated, and then plunged on. "What about HAND, chief?"

"HAND—Humans Against Neuter Domination. I'd almost forgotten about them."

But Jazine knew he hadn't forgotten. None of them had forgotten. Less than a year earlier the revolutionary group known as HAND had struck its first blow against the machine civilization by blowing up the Federal Medical Center in Washington. HAND's former leader, Graham Axman, was safely behind bars as a result of that episode, but many of his followers remained at large, including a youthful escaped exile from the Venus Colony named Euler Frost.

"Wouldn't it be a natural move for HAND to try

6

sabotaging the election computer, chief?"

"But with pre-programming instead of bombs?" Crader was doubtful.

"Sure! Bombs would just destroy it. Something like this pre-programming, if it went undetected till election day, could undermine the people's faith in our entire system. They might even start wondering if President McCurdy was really elected last time."

"Maybe," Crader mused. "Just maybe."

"So what do we do about it?"

Carl Crader activated the desk terminal of his memory bank. "Let's see what the files tell us about the FRIDAY-404." In a moment he had a lengthy printout, which he quickly skimmed. "Lawrence Friday, that's the name I wanted! He developed the entire FRIDAY line. If anyone can tell you about it, he can. Why not call on him and see if he'll shed any light on the matter? Perhaps there's some simple explanation to the whole thing—one that doesn't involve HAND and plots to fix the presidential election."

"Good idea," Jazine agreed. "Where can I find this man Friday?"

Crader consulted his printout once more. "In a most unlikely place. It seems he's now the director of the Central Park Zooitorium."

Earl Jazine liked zoos and always had, ever since his parents had taken him to a zoo in Chicago once to see the last giraffe in the world before it died. That had been nearly twenty years ago, and he'd been going to zoos ever since. Manhattan's Central Park Zooitorium was unique in its construction, however,

7

consisting of a huge bubble dome which covered the entire southern third of the park. Constructed in the pollution era before the advent of electric cars and climate control, the domed zoo had provided perfect contentment for animals of all species. Even the giant pandas, nearly extinct in Russo-China itself, were thriving beneath the plastic pleasure dome.

Jazine wandered the paths to the central administrative office, where he found Professor Lawrence Friday alone in an office that seemed more like a chemist's lab than a zookeeper's study.

"But I'm not a zookeeper, you see," Friday told him in response to Earl's opening comment. "I'm an administrator, and there's quite a difference." He was a slender man of perhaps fifty years, who carried himself with the slightly stoop-shouldered resignation of a person who has bent to some minute task most of his life. Jazine had seen the look before, among scientists at their microscopes and astronomers at their telescopes. Perhaps it was not too strange to find it among computer technicians turned zoo directors.

"In any event," Jazine observed, "it's a hell of a long way from the FRIDAY-404."

Lawrence Friday smiled slightly, in recognition of his brainchild. "Not so far as you'd think, Mr. Jazine. The city and state allow me complete freedom to carry on my experiments here, as long as they do not interfere with my work."

"And what experiments would those be?"

"The nervous system of animals and reptiles as it relates to the computer sciences."

"You must be kidding, Professor!"

8

"Not at all," he replied, smiling slightly as if he'd had this reaction before. "Scientists had the clues a full century ago, during World War II, if they'd only followed through with them. At that time, extensive secret research was conducted into electric eels—but it was aimed at finding an antidote for nerve gas. I have carried that research several steps further, tracing the electrical output of eels and other animals as it relates to the nervous system, and thus to computer sciences. Because, you see, the brain of today's computer is not much different from the brain of a lower animal."

"Interesting," Jazine conceded, not really knowing if the man was talking sense.

"At least it explains my interest in animals and computers," Professor Friday said with a smile. "If that's what roused the curiosity of the Computer Investigation Bureau."

"It wasn't really that, Professor. I came to talk to you about the FRIDAY-404."

"The election unit?" A frown knitted his forehead.

"Correct." Earl ran quickly through the events of the last few days, covering in some detail his investigation of the FRIDAY-404 computer. When he'd finished, he leaned back and asked, "Any ideas?"

Lawrence Friday tapped a pencil against his lower lip. "One thought comes immediately to mind. The FRIDAY-404, like all of the election apparatus, is unused during most of the year. Unused and unguarded. It would be fairly simple for some person or group to gain access to the computer relay stations and through them to the skysphere satellite. Using ordinary computers to cast their ballots, they could

9

then have the voting tabulated by my FRIDAY-404 system and relayed by the satellite to some central point—obviously not Washington."

Earl Jazine thought immediately of HAND. "Are you familiar with a group called Humans Against Neuter Domination?"

"HAND? Of course! I read the telenews like everyone else. In my line of work they could hardly have escaped attention."

"Could HAND be using the FRIDAY-404 for some sort of election, or to sabotage the legitimate presidential elections?"

"It's possible."

"Is there anything about the construction or operation of the FRIDAY-404 that would enable us to backtrack to the source of input? Anything that could pinpoint the approximate time of input?"

"Not really," Friday said. Then he added, "But there is one thing—a memory unit that allows a double-check on returns, to be certain none are reported twice by the same voting machine. This memory unit could tell you whether the figures are new input."

Jazine got to his feet. "That might help us. I'll check it out. You'll be available if we need more help?"

"Certainly."

"Lawrence Friday walked partway out with him, commenting on the new dolphin pool that had just been installed. It was after they parted, as Jazine boarded the moving sidewalk for the Fifth Avenue exit, that he realized he was being followed. The man had blended into the crowd at first, but as the
10

strollers thinned out on the walk he edged his way up, getting closer to where Jazine stood with one hand on the safety rail.

He was a slender man with nondescript features except for an odd tattooed design on his left cheek. He could have been either a private detective or a hired killer, and Jazine was still trying to decide which as the moving sidewalk passed over a little bridge spanning the lion habitat. Then, before he realized what was happening, the man stepped around two children and pulled a stunner gun from under his coat.

Jazine tried to duck, but the force of the weapon caught him full in the chest, knocking him against the safety rail. Then the man's powerful hands were upon him, rolling him over the rail, off the bridge. Still half conscious, Jazine felt himself falling, saw the ground rushing up to meet him.

As he sprawled broken in the grass, he saw the first lion moving toward him.

2.

CARL CRADER

The doctor looked into Crader's questioning eyes and said, "Don't worry. He'll live."

"How bad is it?"

"Two broken ribs and a concussion from the fall, plus a few cuts and bruises, but otherwise he's not bad. We want to keep him hospitalized for a day or so, but then he can go home."

"Are visitors allowed?"

"Sure. Go ahead." The doctor motioned toward the closed door and retreated down the plasticized corridor.

Inside, Crader found Earl Jazine sitting up in bed, swathed in bandages but apparently in good spirits. "Hello, chief," he said, just a bit sheepishly.

Carl Crader eyed the flowers and get-well tele-prints. "One day in the hospital and you acquire all this? Who are the flowers from?"

"Judy, your secretary. She put your name on them too."

Crader grunted and sat down. Judy and Earl were always friendly, and he knew they'd been out to-gether a few times. "How did it happen? When I heard

12

you'd been mauled by a lion at the zooitorium—"

"It wasn't exactly like that," Jazine said, trying to adjust to a more comfortable position in the electronic air-bed. "Somebody was following me. He let go with a stunner blast and then dumped me off a bridge. The lions were the least of my worries. They sniffed around and roared a bit, but that was about all. One of them scratched me with his paw."

"Any idea who tried to kill you?"

Jazine shook his head, then held his hands to his temples. "God, that doesn't feel so good with a concussion! No, I never saw the guy before, chief. But he sure seemed to know I was visiting Lawrence Friday."

"What did Friday have to offer?"

Jazine repeated the conversation as best he could remember it. When he'd finished, Carl Crader said, "A secret election! That's hardly likely."

"Remember how unlikely the transvection machine business was, chief? These are unlikely times. Hell, fifty years ago, the Venus Colony would have seemed unlikely too."

The mention of the Venus Colony reminded Crader of Stanley Ambrose. He'd meant to run a check on the man, just to see what he was up to back on earth. Perhaps, if there was anything to this election idea, he was the Ambrose of Blunt and Ambrose. "All right, Earl, we'll look into it further. It certainly seems you've stumbled onto something, or they wouldn't have tried to kill you. What did he look like—this man with the stunner?"

"Slender, with an odd tattoo on his left cheek." Jazine's bandaged face clouded, as if he was trying to

13

recapture some half-forgotten impression. "His hands were very powerful. I was stunned when he rolled me over that bridge railing, but I still had the impression of powerful hands."

Crader nodded. "I'll run a computer check through Washington and see if they come up with anything."

"Maybe HAND is hiring assassins these days."

"It's not their sort of crime," Crader said. "Remember when Euler Frost tried to kill the secretary of extra-terrestrial defense? He used an anesthesia gun loaded with an industrial poison. Somehow that seems more HAND's way than a stunner gun and a flip into a lion pit."

"That was HAND's way in the past, before they blew up the computers at the Federal Medical Center. Who knows what their way is today?"

A chime sounded on the wall behind Crader and a nurse's recorded voice said, "This patient is under automated care control. Since visits are limited to fifteen minutes, we must request that you now leave."

"The machines again," Crader said with a smile. He got to his feet. "Take it easy now, and don't worry. I'll get right onto this election business and see if there's anything to it."

He left the hospital and took the moving sidewalk to the lot where his electric car was parked. At that moment he had every intention of following through on Earl Jazine's investigation as soon as he returned to his office. But life isn't always that simple.

The offices of the Computer Investigation Bureau at the summit of the World Trade Center were in

14

more than their usual state of confusion when he arrived. Judy had a sheaf of urgent printouts for him, and word that President McCurdy had phoned from the New White House.

"Get the President," Crader decided, because that always came first.

In less than a minute he was facing President Mc-Curdy on the vision-phone. "Carl, good to see you. What's this I hear about one of your men being attacked?"

"Earl Jazine, sir. You've met him in Washington. I just came from the hospital. He shouldn't be laid up more than a few days."

"Yes, yes! But who did it? Is this more of HAND's work?"

"We don't know, sir. We're working on that." Staring at the vigorous gray-haired man on the screen made Carl Crader feel old. In a young man's world, Andrew Jackson McCurdy had survived to his fiftieth year. He was already older than the last three presidents had been when they left office, and now he was running for a third term. Somehow Crader did not want to tell him just then about what Earl had found in that election computer. Not until there was more information. No need of rousing all those sleeping dogs in Washington.

"Well, we have another problem," President Mc-Curdy said, quickly changing the subject. A month before election, there were always many problems. Anything that might upset a sector of the electorate became a problem.

"What's that, sir?"

"Radiation leakage out in Chicago. You should

15

have a scan on it. The telenews has been playing it up all day."

"Computer-caused?"

"I wouldn't be calling on you if it wasn't," President McCurdy rapped back, just a bit testily. "Get right on it, will you? The people get in a panic whenever there's radiation leakage."

"Yes, sir," Crader replied, and the screen before him went blank. The President had broken the connection. Crader picked up the sheaf of printouts and tried to read through them, but the words kept blurring. Once again McCurdy had made him realize he was getting old. A few more years and they'd force him out at sixty-five. There was no more staying on till you were seventy-seven, as Hoover had done in the last century.

"Judy!" he called into the intercom.

"I'm here." She appeared at his office door.

"Judy, my eyes are tired. Give me a rundown on this Chicago radiation business, will you?"

"Certainly." She took the papers from his hand and asked, a bit too casually, "How's Earl?"

Crader had to smile. He'd forgotten to give her a report. "Concussion and some broken ribs, but he'll be out of the hospital in a few days. He liked your flowers."

She blushed prettily. "They were from the office."

"Now then, what about Chicago?" He leaned back and closed his eyes, listening.

"High radiation levels on the South Side, with no apparent source. The only industry nearby is Crossway Computers. They make these little deskpacks for accountants to use at home. But they insist
16

there's no radiation involved."

"What's the power source of the deskpacks?"

"Regular wall outlets, the same as adding machines a century ago. Not much progress there."

"But President McCurdy thought the radiation was computer-caused."

"Remember the radiation scandal of 2024?" Judy was great on history.

"You were barely born then!" He opened his eyes long enough to admire her crossed legs, enticingly blue in the bodysuit which government employees had finally been allowed to wear on the job.

"I read about it, though!" she countered defensively.

"Do people still read?"

"I do! Those video cassettes drive me up the wall after a while."

"Glad to hear it. Sometimes they affect me the same way. Now where were we?"

"The scandal of 2024, when a radiation leak in the Lake Superior reactor almost canceled the federation of the United States and Canada. That one cost Abraham Burke a second term as president. I don't suppose McCurdy wants history repeated."

"Anybody die in Chicago?"

"Not yet, but three children are in critical condition. They all live in the neighborhood."

"What are the levels of Alpha-particle emissions?"

She read him a series of figures, ending with the observation, "The measurements were all taken from the air. The radiation is almost certainly airborne."

"Does Crossway Computers have smokeless stacks?"

17

"Of course! It's the law. But you know that doesn't screen out radiation, chief."

He opened his eyes once more. "Get me a screen-map of the area. Order it up on our map table." He walked across the room to the flat table of frosted plastic, about the size of a skull-pool game. There, after only a moment's wait, he saw a detailed photo-map of Chicago's South Side.

"This is the area of radiation," Judy said, circling several blocks with a neon pencil. "The computer plant is here, near the center."

Crader grunted and studied the map. "Then the plant is not at fault."

"Why not?"

"Prevailing winds are from the west. The radiation, if it's airborne as you say, would tend to drift downwind. No, I think we'll find its source over here, on the western edge of your circle."

"But there's nothing there. No industry."

"What's this building?" he asked, pointing to a white rectangle with a smokeless stack on top.

Judy consulted the coordinate list. "Mains Brothers. A crematorium."

"Of course," Crader said softly, letting out his breath. "It had to be."

"Be what? It only burns bodies, and they're not radioactive."

"Not usually, but in this case I'll bet they are. Last year nearly a million Americans were implanted with heart and brain pacemakers powered by plutonium capsules. Theoretically, all crematoriums are supposed to check with the medical registry in Washington before burning a body, so that any such atomic

18

device can be removed first. But in actual practice they sometimes slip up. It appears that the Mains Brothers have been slipping up a great deal."

"Here's the reason," Judy said, checking her coordinates again. "They're only three blocks from the Sunnyside Rest Pavilion, and they're getting all the old people who die—the ones most likely to have implanted pacemakers."

Crader flipped off the viewing table lights. "That's it, then. Contact the Health Bureau in Washington and fill them in. It's their baby now, not ours."

The day entangled Carl Crader in such a variety of tasks that it was late afternoon before he again remembered the election computer and the names of Blunt and Ambrose. He ran a check on his desk unit and found there were two Jason Blunts and four Stanley Ambroses in the master file:

Jason Blunt, astronomer, New York City
Jason Blunt, oilman, Gulf of Mexico
Stanley Ambrose, space lawyer, Philadelphia
Stanley Ambrose, clone biologist, Paris
Stanley Ambrose, retired director of Venus Colony,
Address Unknown
Stanley Ambrose, naturalist, Polar Colony

Crader scanned the list and sighed with frustration. "We need more information, Judy. If there was a secret election of some sort, the candidates could have been any of the men on this list—or any of a hundred other Blunts or Ambroses we know nothing about."

"But if thousands of people voted for them, even secretly, they must be well known," Judy said.

19

"True enough." He pondered the list again. "Stanley Ambrose's present address is unknown, according to this. In fact, I've heard nothing about him since he retired from the Venus Colony. That might be significant. If he's gone with HAND or some other secret group, he may have dropped from sight."

"What about Jason Blunt? There are only two on the list."

"That might be easier to pin down, provided we can believe the computer that there are only two Jason Blunts well-known in public life."

"Our memory bank includes all listings in every major biographical reference work. Blunt is not that common a name."

"Very well. Let's try the local Mr. Blunt first. The astronomer."

It took Judy only a few minutes to locate Blunt and put in a vision-phone call. She returned shaking her head. "He's eighty-two years old and confined to a rest home upstate. I think we can cross him off the list."

Crader nodded. "That leaves Jason Blunt, the oilman. Know anything about him?"

"I can find out."

He glanced at the digital wall clock. "It's pretty late now, Judy, I suppose it can wait till tomorrow."

It had been a long day, and he could see she wasn't about to argue with him. As she retreated to the outer office he spun around in his chair to gaze out at the Jersey flatlands and the distant Nixon International Jetport. The sun was low in the western sky, a reminder that autumn had begun and the long winter

20

nights would soon be upon them. Crader wished that daylight could be controlled somehow, the way the climate was. He enjoyed the winters almost completely free of snow, and the summers when most showers came at night. This night, like many others, he'd putter a bit in his suburban garden. Perhaps he might even help his wife plant a new crop of winter flowers. If only there was a bit more daylight . . .

"Mr. Crader, I thought you should see this."

He pulled himself back to the present and glanced up at Judy. Her face was white as she held an urgent message-form out to him. "It just came through."

He scanned the words quickly. *"Computer engineer Harry Rogers slain in office. Unknown man hunted."*

"Rogers?" He looked up quizzically.

"Rogers was the man who first reported the irregularities with the FRIDAY-404 election computer. He's the one Earl talked to."

"All right," Crader said, suddenly decisive. "It looks as if we work late tonight after all. Get me that printout on Jason Blunt, and send Mike Sabin over to the hospital to stay with Earl. They just might have another try at him."

3.
MASHA BLUNT

Her name originally was Masha Konya, and she'd grown up in one of the thriving industrial cities of central Turkey. But she'd never been fully content there, not since she was twelve and a boy tried to rape her and she realized in a full flash of illumination that she was both beautiful and desirable.

After that, the city of her childhood was too small for her. Masha left home before her fifteenth birthday and journeyed to New Istanbul, a gleaming city of towers and bridges that straddled the Bosporus like some twenty-first-century Colossus of Rhodes. She dreamed of dancing in the great golden pleasure mosques, where wealthy men from all over the world came to gamble and sin. This was to be the life for her—not the stifling regularity of an industrial city, where she might end her days with festering lungs and flabby thighs.

The entrepreneurs of New Istanbul were quick to recognize Masha Konya's charms. A man named Fizel arranged for her to study the nearly forgotten art of belly dancing, and by the time of her fifteenth birthday she was working nights in a little club called The Last Century, dancing and hustling drinks between numbers. That was where she met a man named Stevro and, later, Jason Blunt.

In a very real sense, Stevro won Masha from Fizel one night over the gaming tables. They were playing electronic roulette for thousand-dollar chips, and when Fizel's money ran short Stevro offered to stake him, in exchange for the young dancer Masha. In the heat of the moment Fizel agreed, certain he would win back his money and the girl. He didn't, and that night after the last show Stevro collected his prize.

Masha was fearful of Stevro at first. He was a bulky, jerky sort of man with a habit of smoking soilweed, a synthetic, mind-expanding drug much used in the Near East. Gazing down at Masha as she sat on the edge of the bed that first night, he said, "You are very beautiful, my dear. Very beautiful indeed."

She already knew what he wanted, and she started to remove her dancer's costume. "I belonged to Fizel," she said. "You had no right to take me."

He inhaled on the harsh little soilweed cigar, and his eyes seemed to glaze over a bit. At first she thought the drug was getting to him and that she would sleep alone at least for this night. But then as the last of her garments fell away he put down the cigar and stepped back to fully admire her naked beauty.

"Yes," he said softly. "And how old are you, my dear?"

"Fifteen."

"How many men have you been with?"

"A boy back home, and Fizel, and two of his customers. That is all."

"Are you wise in the ways of lovemaking? Do you know the functions of the solanum, and the electric lance, and the pigeon eggs?"

"I . . . no," she admitted. "It has always been the same, except for the last man. He wanted to beat me first, before we made love."

"I will teach you," he said. "I will teach you all there is to know. And someday you will sail away on one of those big atomic yachts that harbor here. You'd like that, wouldn't you?"

"Yes."

"We will begin tomorrow."

He came to her then, very gently, as if he were handling valuable merchandise. He came to her, and took her in a way she had not known before.

The very next day, strolling with Stevro along the docks where the big yachts berthed, she heard him begin his course of instruction.

"You see, my dear, there are very wealthy men who own these ships. Some of them have made their money in space exploration, or in undersea oil wells. They are men of middle age, often already married and divorced. They come here to New Istanbul to recapture their lost youth, most often in the arms of a young girl like yourself. But you have seen those pigs who work for Fizel. No rich man could bear the sight of them for more than a single night. You, my dear, you are different. To possess you, a man would even marry you."

"Marry?"

Stevro nodded. "I am not training you to be some rich man's mistress, my dear. I am training you for a

24

wifely role."

And for a year Stevro did just that. She attended ballet classes and studied the space sciences by day, learning all there was to know about the life around them in the middle of the twenty-first century. ("Wealthy men are most interested in space," Stevro explained.) Then by night he took over her education personally, initiating her in the many ways of love and lust, showing her how the beauty of her body could be used to please one man.

"This," he told her one night, "is solanum, a form of nightshade which can serve as a powerful aphrodisiac. When your husband is low, a bit of this will rouse his spirits without fail."

"I see," she said, fingering the dusky powder.

"And here is an electric lance. Have you ever seen one before?"

"No." She stared wide-eyed at the smooth plastic rod, imagining it penetrating her.

"Male prostitutes sometimes use them. And nymphomaniacs, of course. The tip delivers a series of gentle electric shocks."

"How ghastly!"

"In a sense it is, because it is one more mechanization of life. But you see, my dear, we must take advantage of these tools as long as they are offered to us. If the husband I choose for you is too elderly to perform with satisfaction, you might welcome a little help from the electric lance."

"Never! I would never marry such a man!"

He sighed and lit another of his soilweed cigars. "How old are you now, Masha dear?"

"Sixteen."

"Yes, sixteen." He stared out into space for a moment, as if calculating the rate of return on some investment. Then he said, "It is time we began looking for a husband."

At the electronic casino, Masha soon became a regular sight. She would arrive on the arm of Stevro, dressed in some expensive and radiant costume that could not fail to attract attention. Her favorite among these was a long white gown of moondust, slit from neck to ankles, which fell open at every movement to reveal the pale pink bodysuit beneath. She especially liked its effect on men, liked the way their mouths dropped open when she entered a room for the first time.

She was wearing the moondust gown on the night she first met Jason Blunt. He was not the first of the millionaires to whom Stevro had been attracted, but he was the first to show real promise. Just two nights earlier, while displaying Masha's charms to a visiting Frenchman, Stevro had been forced to break the man's arm when he attempted to pull her away into his car.

Jason Blunt was nothing like the Frenchman. He was an American for one thing, and Masha had known very few of those. She guessed his age at about forty-five, though at the swimming pool and in the gym he displayed the muscles and endurance of a much younger man. His long black hair and trim beard were only beginning to streak with gray, and there was a twinkle about his eyes that made Masha hope from the moment she met him that he would be the one.

As the moondust gown fell away from her thighs, she saw the interest in his face, and when she happened to make some intelligent comment on the state of the Venus Colony with its continuing rivalry between the Americans and the Russo-Chinese, he reached out to touch her hand in a gesture of agreement.

"You know a great deal for one so young and charming," he said.

"I had a good teacher." She raised her eyes to Stevro, who at times like this never left her side.

Perhaps something in her look caused Jason Blunt to turn his head toward the bulky man with his short, foul-smelling cigars. He nodded slightly, as if he understood everything.

The following night, Blunt and Stevro dined alone while Masha anxiously awaited the verdict in her room. When Stevro joined her shortly before midnight he was smiling, and she knew it would be all right. "He wishes to spend one night with you, my dear, to verify the truth of all that I told him. If he finds I have not lied, he is prepared to pay one million American dollars for your hand in marriage."

"A million . . ."

"A small sum to him. One day's output of his undersea oil wells."

"But to pay so much for *me*!"

Stevro came up to where she sat and ran his pudgy fingers through her hair. "You are more than worth it, my dear. Never forget, wherever life may take you, that I taught you what you know. You're a pupil of Stevro, and that's something to be proud of."

"But if Jason Blunt marries me, what will you do?"

He shrugged and looked away. "Go back to Fizel's, I suppose, and find another like you. If such a thing is possible."

Her night with Jason Blunt was more than successful, as she knew in her newfound confidence it would be. The following morning he presented Stevro with a certified check for one million dollars, and that afternoon Masha and Jason were married in the New Church of the Moon, overlooking the Bosporus. That evening they sailed with the tide and were carried into the becalmed waters of the Mediterranean on a honeymoon voyage.

When they had been at sea five days, Masha looked up from her sunning mat and asked, "Jason, were you ever married before?"

He was exercising nude on the top deck of the atomic yacht *Strombol,* and he waited until he had lowered himself from the parallel bars before answering. "Few men in my position reach the age of forty-five without a wife or two along the way. But they were nothing like you, Masha."

"I was just curious."

"There were two. Both are gone now." She did not know if he meant dead or merely divorced, and she did not ask him.

"Stevro said you are very wealthy."

He chuckled at that, flexing thigh muscles as he bent to lift a hundred-pound weight. She could not help admiring the curve of his naked body, remembering how he had held her just a few hours earlier.

28

"Yes," he answered. "I am very wealthy. Next week we will dock at one of my man-made islands, where the oil drilling is carried on. Then you will see what real wealth is!"

"You said you lived on an island."

"I live on many islands, all of which I own. My home base is the man-made island of Sargasso."

"In the Atlantic?"

"No, though in a way it was named for the one-time Sargasso Sea. When that calm area of seaweed-infested ocean became clogged with pollution—bits of plastic, beer cans, logs, everything—around the turn of the century, it was my father who helped clear it out. He owned a marine salvage company, one of the best in the business at the time, and the sea-rail companies hired him to do the job. With the profits from it, he built the island of Sargasso in the Gulf of Mexico, and it was there that he drilled his first undersea oil well. You see, Sargasso and these other places are drilling islands—floating islands, anchored in place—whose primary function is the location and production of oil from undersea beds. There are dozens of them now, and they have made me very wealthy."

"Is your father alive?"

"No. He and my mother have been dead for years." He put down the weight. "But that is enough family history for one day. We're on our honeymoon, remember?"

She rolled over on the mat, welcoming him to her.

Masha's first glimpse of Sargasso was a bit startling. Somehow she'd envisioned it as a sunny plantation in the middle of the sea, with rolling lawns and a big white twentieth-century house. She'd even imagined that the yacht would be met by hundreds of workingmen, their faces dabbed in oil, who'd turn out to welcome the master home.

When she told Jason Blunt of her dream, he merely scoffed. "This is no old-time cotton plantation, girl. The drilling is fully automated, done by machine. Except for a handful of technicians and personal servants, we are alone on the island."

The following day he showed her around the place, starting with the big glass-and-steel cube that was their home. She had never been in such a house, where buttons controlled everything, where video cameras recorded every move and fed pre-programmed signals to the kitchen computer or the recreation computer or the health computer. She had only to rise from bed in the morning and her video image was enough to prepare the orange juice and eggs and coffee before she'd reached the kitchen. She had only to sneeze and the sound of it electronically adjusted the purity of the air to guard against pollutants.

The drilling platform itself was much the same. It was a world without workers, where intricate machines pumped the oil and shipped it off by sea-rail to the great refineries along the Gulf Coast. A few computer technologists and a handful of personal servants were the only people she ever saw, and she often wondered if they were present merely to divert her while Jason was away from the island on his frequent business trips.

It was a boring life at times, but there were compensations. At least twice a year they cruised around the world on the atomic yacht *Strombol,* inspecting the other drilling islands, and in the spring there was a trip to Paris to attend a world meeting of oilmen. She settled into this routine, with occasional trips to New York or Los Angeles, and became a loving, faithful wife to Jason Blunt. She was all that Stevro promised, and more, even learning the role of charming hostess when Jason began to hold his mysterious meetings on the island.

Masha had been married to Jason for three years, and thus she was nineteen when the sea-rail deposited a gray-haired visitor at the island one sunny afternoon in early October.

She went down from the glass-and-steel cube to meet him as a good hostess should, imagining him to be one more of Jason's shadowy associates. "I am Masha Blunt," she said, extending her hand. "Jason should be returning shortly. Are you a business associate of his?"

The gray-haired man, who must have been over sixty years old, smiled down at her. "Not exactly, Ms. Blunt. I've come down from New York to ask him a few questions. My name is Carl Crader, and I'm with the Computer Investigation Bureau."

4.
EARL JAZINE

He was still limping a bit when he left the elevator at the 110th floor and waved hello to Judy. "Thanks for the flowers."

"Good to have you back from the lion pit," she said with a grin. "How're you feeling?"

"My ribs are taped up and my head's not quite right, and I sprained my ankle. Otherwise I'm fine. Is the chief in?"

"The chief is out of town," she informed him. "Gone to the Gulf of Mexico to check on one Jason Blunt."

"The Blunt from the election computer?"

"We think so. He's had a half-dozen people on the case since we learned about Rogers."

"What about Rogers?" Jazine lowered himself into a convenient chair by her desk.

"Sorry, I thought you knew. Somebody entered his office and killed him three days ago. He was shot at close range with a stunner on maximum power."

"So that's why Sabin was sticking so close to me at the hospital! Was it the same guy who tried to feed me to the lions?"

"We think so. A secretary who worked for Rogers

described him as a nondescript man, except for a tattoo on his left cheek."

"That's him," Jazine agreed. "Somebody's trying to stop this whole investigation."

Judy nodded. She'd used some of the new glowon makeup this morning, a variation of the old flippie cult colors, and Jazine found it oddly attractive. "That's not all, Earl. After he killed Rogers, he apparently took the time to electromagnetize the FRIDAY-404 memory cells. The computer was wiped clean of all reference to the Blunt-Ambrose election."

Somehow the news didn't surprise him. The only real surprise was that the tattooed man had bungled with him and left him still alive. "How did the chief get a line on Blunt?"

"There were only two Jason Blunts listed in the names registry, and the other one is eighty-two years old."

"It could be an unknown—some Jason Blunt from Kansas that nobody ever heard of before."

Judy shook her head. "The chief and I reasoned that if there really is a secret election to HAND or some other underground group, the candidates would have to be known well enough within that group. Since the use of the FRIDAY-404 implies a nationwide election, we're looking for someone of nationwide prominence. Jason Blunt seems to fit. We did a quick check on him and discovered he lives on a drilling island in the Gulf of Mexico. Especially interesting is the fact that the island has been the scene of a number of meetings during the past year."

Jazine perked up. "What sort of meetings?"

33

"That's what the chief went to find out."

"Christ, couldn't he have sent Sabin, or waited till I was out of the hospital? It might be dangerous."

"Jason Blunt is a wealthy man. A mere investigator might get nowhere with him, but he could hardly be rude to the director of the CIB."

"Maybe," But he wasn't happy. Perhaps it was just being left out of the investigation that troubled him. "What about the other name—Ambrose?"

"We have four Stanley Ambroses on the list. You can tackle them if you'd like."

He accepted the sheet of paper she gave him. Four names. "This Ambrose's whereabouts are unknown?"

"That's right. The chief thought it strange too."

He remembered a random line in a twentieth-century book by a man named Charles Fort, written after the disappearance of Ambrose Bierce and Ambrose Small. *Was somebody collecting Ambroses?* He left Judy at her desk and spent the rest of the morning checking computer printouts on the four listed men. There was nothing suspicious about any of them—except for the one Stanley Ambrose's seeming disappearance after retiring from the Venus Colony a year earlier.

This Ambrose was a man of fifty-six years, active in government and space matters, who'd served five years as director of the USAC Venus Colony. He'd accomplished much with the domed cities of Venus, changing their entire concept from that of a penal colony to a new frontier. Although the population of the Russo-Chinese Venus Colony still exceeded that of the USAC sector, under Ambrose's farsighted direction there was hope at last that the Americans might someday emerge as the planet's dominant force.

Earl Jazine pondered all this, and decided this Ambrose was the best place to begin. He had no wife or family living, and the Washington file showed only one close friend back on earth—a woman named Mildred Norris who'd been his mistress in the years prior to his Venus assignment. She seemed the only link to the missing Ambrose. It took him another hour to locate her present address, in the medium-sized planned community of Sunsite, Ohio.

That was just an hour away by rocketcopter.

Jazine had never visited Sunsite before, but he'd been in dozens of planned communities amazingly like it. There was always the town square, a throw-back to colonial days, with the town hall on one side, a courthouse opposite, and a church between. The fact that the church was only sparsely attended made no difference to the community planners, who felt it to be an integral part of the American scene.

From this center radiated the streets of the community, striking out like the spokes of a wheel, inter-secting every quarter-mile with cross-streets where shopping plazas and community centers and even an amusement park blossomed. From the air, the town of Sunsite seemed like a giant spider's web—or more accurately, thought Jazine, like a computer's core unit. More accurately, because Sunsite and the other communities like it were the ultimate in compu-terized living. Everything from traffic lights to tele-printers were controlled by machine. Even the goods on the supermarket shelves were carefully inventoried by computers that electronically printed out reorders whenever the supply of an item dropped below a pre-programmed level. And most people ate computerized meals right in their offices.

In such a place, Jazine was not surprised to find Mildred Norris, the woman he sought, working as a computer programmer in the local tax office. He often thought that half the people in America must be employed in programming computers that regulated the lives of the other half.

She was a slim, pretty woman in her early thirties, with hair dyed a soft blue in keeping with a fad of some months back. Her mouth had a sad softness about it that seemed always about to break into a smile, and he could imagine men striving mightily for the reward of that smile.

"Ms. Norris, my name is Earl Jazine. I'm with the Computer Investigation Bureau."

The smile came easily. "Computer Cops."

"That's what the papers call us sometimes."

"What do you want here? Somebody complaining about their taxes?"

"No, it's nothing like that. Actually, I wanted to ask you about Stanley Ambrose."

The smile faded. "That was six years ago. Your records must be very complete."

"They are." He glanced around the sterile white room. "Where can we talk?"

"I'll be finished for the day in twenty minutes. If you want to hear about Stanley Ambrose, you'll have to buy me a drink."

"Good enough. I'll meet you outside at four

36

thirty."

She came out with two other girls, younger than herself, and left them to join Jazine. "Here I am, right on time!"

"Know a place where we can get that drink?"

"There's an automated bar just down the street, if you don't mind your drinks being mixed by machine."

"I'm used to it. If the mix is bad I'll arrest them," he said with a grin.

The place was no better or worse than a hundred others he'd been in. He bought four large metal tokens as they entered, and dropped two of them in the table slot to order Scotch for himself and a bleaker cocktail for Mildred Norris. The drinks were machine-mixed at the bar and delivered to the table by a little automated cart that moved along a track in the floor.

"The drinks are good enough here," she explained by way of apology, "and the tokens don't cost much. I come here with the people from the office sometimes."

"Nice place," he commented, looking around.

"And the police are very good about checking for drunks and under-sixteens." She sipped her cocktail. "Now what did you want to know about Stanley Ambrose?"

"To start with, where is he?"

"I don't know. I haven't seen him in six years."

"Not at all?"

"Not at all. You must know that I was his mistress. He was teaching at the university here, and his wife was dead. It seemed a natural relationship,

37

even though he was old enough to be my father. Marriage was never really discussed. It was simply a convenient relationship for us both. Then, because of his Washington contacts and his writings on space, he was offered the position as director of the Venus Colony. It was too good a job to turn down. We talked about it, and he made a half-hearted offer to marry me and take me along, but frankly I just didn't want to go. The thought of living for five years beneath a big plastic dome on another planet didn't appeal to me."

"So you parted."

She gave a little nod. "It was the best way, really. At first he wrote me every week, and it was fun getting letters from Venus. But that gradually slacked off and stopped about two years ago. Of course I read in the telenews that he was back on earth, but I've heard nothing from him."

"And you've no idea where he might be?"

"None whatever."

"What about his politics, Ms. Norris?"

"You can call me Milly. Everyone does." The smile was back.

"Milly."

"We talked very little about politics, though he occasionally mentioned something about it in his letters from Venus."

"Did you keep those letters?"

"Yes."

"Could I see them?"

"They're at my apartment. I suppose I could show them to you."

"Good." He downed the rest of his drink and
38

started to get up.

She stared at him in some surprise. "You bought four tokens. Don't I get my other drink first?"

"Oh! Sure, you do." He dropped the tokens into the table slot and repeated the order.

"You're not like him a bit, you know," she said, studying Jazine.

"Like who?"

"Stanley Ambrose."

"I hope not. I'm a quarter-century younger, for one thing."

"I don't mean just that. You're a very down-to-earth person, aren't you?"

"Sometimes."

"Married?"

"No. My job takes me all over the world. It wouldn't be fair to a wife."

"An old bachelor's excuse!"

"Maybe, but it really is dangerous. A man with a tattooed cheek tried to kill me just a few days ago." He told her about it as the drinks arrived on their little cart. But he made the story short. If Milly Norris was preparing to seduce him, he wasn't about to waste time with too many preliminaries.

Her apartment was neat and compact, something like the woman herself. It overlooked one of the community playgrounds scatter-sited throughout the town, but otherwise he could say little for the view. The land was flat in all directions, with only occasional trees to break up the rigid conformity of the structures.

As if reading his thoughts, she said, "The better

39

homes are on the outskirts. This is a middle-income zone here."

"Very nice," he mumbled.

"It serves its purpose. A place to sleep and eat."

He walked over to scan the video cassettes on her shelves. They were mostly romance and sex titles like *Girl in Free-Fall, Rocket Rendezvous, Twenty-first-Century Morals, Dressing to Attract a Man,* and *New Bedroom Techniques Illustrated.*

"I used to watch those when I was young," she said over his shoulder by way of explanation. "How about a drink?"

"Fine. Scotch'll do, if you have it."

She returned in a moment with the glass. "Here you are—poured by hand!"

"That's the way I like it best. Do you have those letters handy?" He always believed in disposing of the business first.

Milly rummaged around in the closetier and came up with a thin packet of envelopes bearing the stamp of the Interplanetary Postal Service. Jazine glanced through them quickly, looking for the political comments he sought.

They were few and superficial for the most part, but in one of the last letters, written two years earlier, there was a paragraph that caught his eye: *"The videonews may have reported on our recent troubles here. A young prisoner named Euler Frost escaped from the colony and was living illegally in the Free Zone with some Russo-Chinese. But he's been recaptured now, along with his friends, and things are peaceful once again."*

Euler Frost was one of the leaders of HAND, and

though Jazine had never met him, he knew Crader had encountered the man twice during the transvection affair. After fleeing from the Venus Colony, Frost had joined Graham Axman in HAND's attack on the Federal Medical Center. The paragraph in Ambrose's letter wasn't much, but it was at least a link between the missing man and someone in the HAND organization.

"This might help," he told Milly. "Can I copy it?"

"Sure. He stopped the personal stuff long before that."

Jazine spread the letter flat and photocopied it with his pocket microfilmer. "Thanks. This could prove helpful."

"Helpful. That's me."

"What about his colleagues at the university? Might any of them know his whereabouts?"

"I doubt if he kept in touch with any of them."

"And he has no family?"

She shook her head. "He was a man who believed in a small but intimate circle of friends. Want to see his hologram?"

"We have some on file, but I'd be interested in any candid shots you might have."

"I tried to get him to sit for a formal hologram portrait, but he never would. These are just a few candids taken at a university picnic before he left for Venus."

Earl Jazine stared at the shots of a well-built, ruddy man with wild white hair. There were the usual holograms of him drinking beer and eating, and even pitching a fine left-handed softball during a game. Jazine made quick two-dimensional copies of them all, because he never knew what Crader might want to see.

"You've been a great help to me," he told Milly.

"You're not going so soon!"

He grinned at the invitation in her eyes. "No, as a matter of fact I thought I might stay a bit longer if you've no objection."

She turned on the video to a blank channel and the apartment filled with lush stereo music. "Romantic," she said. "It's the way people made love a hundred years ago."

"Don't they still do it to music today?"

"Maybe in New York, in the noise zones. Here in Sunsite it's always quiet." She touched a plastic ziplock and her dress fell away. The bodysuit beneath it was a shimmer of radiance at the breasts and groin. Jazine had read about such suits, but this was his first personal experience with one.

"Very nice," was all he could say. His mouth was quite dry.

"The bedroom's in here, Earl."

He followed her nude into the cycled bed and waited while she adjusted the speed in time with the music. Then, as he reached out to touch her smooth waiting skin, he felt her tense beneath his fingertips. "What is it?"

"The outer door—someone's in the apartment!"

He started out of the bed, but it was already too late. Three men, masked and carrying stunners, crowded into the bedroom. "Don't move," the leader barked, pointing his weapon at Jazine's groin, "or you won't live to enjoy that!"

Tied and blindfolded, Jazine was quickly carried out of the apartment to a waiting car. He had no way of knowing whether Milly Norris was also a prisoner, but he suspected she was. He wasn't ready to consider the possibility that she'd lured him into a trap.

The electric car purred silently along to its destination, coming to a smooth stop after what Jazine judged had been an hour's drive. He was bundled roughly into a building of some sort, and the blindfold removed from his eyes.

"You are Earl Jazine of the Computer Investigation Bureau?" one of the masked men demanded.

"Yes," he admitted, blinking his eyes against the glare of an arc light directed at his face.

They'd allowed him to dress, but somehow he still felt naked and helpless before their unseen faces. "Are you aware of your crimes against society?" a voice asked.

"What crimes are those?"

"You have been judged and found guilty by a people's revolutionary court. The sentence is death."

Jazine tried to rise, but several hands restrained him. His arms were still bound to his sides, and he knew he was helpless against the fate they'd prepared for him. "Then get it over with," he said, spitting at the light.

"Your death will not be as fast as all that. You will be sealed in a plastic tube and dropped down a mine shaft with radioactive waste materials. There you will have some days to ponder your fate as the radioactivity eats away at your bones and blood."

Mine shaft. He knew that must mean a salt mine, where such waste products were regularly disposed

43

of. He tried to recall maps of the Sunsite area, and finally pinpointed a group of abandoned salt mines about an hour north of the city. Just then, he couldn't imagine what good the knowledge would do him.

Rough hands seized him once again, and he was lifted into a smooth plastic tube about the size of a coffin. It was indeed a waste disposal tube for radioactive material, and for the first time Jazine felt the sting of fear. "Where's the woman?" he managed to ask. "Is she safe?"

There was no answer, and then the lid was slammed shut on him. He tried to work his arms free of the straps, fighting now for his life, but it was useless. He felt the tube being attached to some conveyor belt, and in another moment he was sliding down a long chute into the bowels of the earth.

For some minutes after the disposal tube came to rest at the base of the mine shaft, Jazine was afraid to move. He imagined himself surrounded by deadly radioactive material which might somehow hasten his end if he exerted himself. Finally, when he decided that was foolish, he set to work freeing his arms. It took him a half hour of effort to achieve it, and even then his arms were so sore and limp as to be virtually helpless. His fingers clawed at the sealed plastic lid, but it failed to move. Freeing his hands had been no help at all.

He tried to feel around for some tool or weapon which might have been left inside the tube, but there was nothing. He was utterly alone with his fate. Feeling through his pockets he was surprised to find the

44

little microfilm camera still intact, along with his money and credit cards. They were honest murderers, at least.

The air within the tube was beginning to grow stale, and the thought crossed his mind that he might easily suffocate before the radiation killed him. It would be a faster way, at any rate, if no more pleasant.

Then he heard a sound.

Only a nibble of sound at first, as if a rat had clawed at the plastic casing.

He heard it again, louder.

Something, or someone, was outside his plastic shell, gnawing at it. Suddenly he realized it was a drill of some sort, slipping as it sought to penetrate the smooth surface.

It took hold at last, humming and hewing, until a tiny hole appeared in the surface of his shell. He saw light from a torch, and he shouted encouragement. "I'm in here! Hurry up!"

More holes cut through the material, bracketing the door hinges, and in another few moments the lid fell away. Earl Jazine breathed a long sigh of relief and clambered out of his coffin.

The man with the torch and drill was young, with a handsome face and deep-set eyes. Jazine recognized him at once from a hologram he'd seen once in the Washington files.

"Euler Frost, isn't it?" he said, holding out his hand. "I guess I owe you my life."

5.

EULER FROST

Perhaps the most important and formative event in Euler Frost's thirty years on earth and Venus had been the death of his father, cut down by a rocket-copter's exhaust blast as he attempted to prevent a mineral survey of Indian land in Manitoba. That event, when Euler was only fourteen, had turned him into a revolutionary. A passive revolutionary at first, but a revolutionary nonetheless. His father had taught him a fear and distrust of all machines, and had punctuated the lesson by the manner of his death.

Exiled to the Venus Colony for membership in a nameless, leaderless group opposed to the dehumanization of the individual in an increasingly machine-dominated society, Euler Frost had escaped from the domed city to live with outcasts like himself in the Free Zone between the USAC and Russo-Chinese sectors. There he encountered tragedy for the second time when raiding troops killed Fergana, a girl he'd grown to love. Frost had slain one of the soldiers in return, and been sentenced to a maximum-security prison on the planet.

His escape from the prison and his arrival back on

earth at a time when the Computer Cops were investigating the murder of a cabinet member had made him a prime suspect in that killing. Alone and friendless, hunted by the police, he'd found a home with HAND, the revitalized organization to which he'd belonged in his youth. HAND's leader, Graham Axman, wasted no talk on slogans or demonstrations. His goal was the utter destruction of the machine-oriented society, by whatever means possible.

The first blow struck by HAND had been a raid on the Federal Medical Center and the destruction of the nation's largest known computer complex. Though Crader and Jazine blunted the force of the attack and captured Graham Axman, Frost and a few others made good their escape. Frost knew it was Carl Crader who allowed him to escape, and now as he reached out to shake the hand of Crader's assistant he wondered if the director of the CIB might consider the debt paid.

"We'd better get out of here," he told Earl Jazine. "The place is loaded with radioactivity."

"How did you find me?"

"It wasn't easy," Frost said, shining his light on an emergency stairway that ran along the chute. "I followed them when they kidnapped you, but I lost them for a time out here at the mines."

"Then it wasn't HAND that tried to kill me?"

"No more than it was the first time, at the zooitorium."

"You seem to know everything."

"I know a great deal. Come on now—up these stairs."

There was no time for further talk until they'd made the climb and regained their breath. Then, in Frost's car, Jazine said, "I was with a woman—Milly Norris. We have to find her."

"They released her on a country road, unharmed. You're the one they were after."

"Why me?"

"Because you stumbled onto the election computer and the names of Blunt and Ambrose. Let me tell you a story. It may sound fantastic, but I can assure you every word is true."

"I'm listening."

"After HAND's raid on the Federal Medical Center I went into hiding. There were still a few of us left, but with Graham Axman sentenced to a long prison term we were like a body without its brain. I tried to take over, holding the group together, and before many months I discovered we had a foe every bit as deadly as the federal government and the Computer Cops."

"Who would that be?" Jazine asked, his curiosity obviously aroused.

"There exists in this country a well-financed conspiracy to overthrow the government of President McCurdy or his successor, and to replace it with a super-government run by computers."

"Fantastic!"

"Of course. But the men behind the plan really believe in it. They have assembled the largest network of computers in the nation—far more than those we destroyed at the Federal Medical Center— and into these computers they have fed every available fact and statistic on American life and history.

One whole memory bank is given over to the stock market, another to elections, a third to foreign policy, and so forth. These computers, by weighing past performance against present conditions, will regulate every aspect of our lives."

"But why? To what purpose?"

"The men behind this—wealthy and powerful in their own right—believe such a computerized government is the only way to preserve our American way of life. You see, the computers will elect new presidents, and regulate the stock market's ups and downs, and even write treaties with other nations— but all this will be within the limits pre-programmed into the machine, limits carefully established by the past. The super-government wants us merely to relive that past—with only minor computerized variations to make it interesting."

"You can't be serious!" Jazine said. "The people would never stand for such a thing!"

"Wouldn't they? The supporters of the super-government could be quite articulate in pointing out its advantages—a balanced budget every year, an equitable sharing of the tax burden, an end to any lingering racial discrimination, no more recessions, no more inflation. Everything would be regulated by the computers. Best of all, from their standpoint, it would insure the American way of life for all time. There would be no chance for communism or any other ism to ever gain a foothold here."

"What about free will?"

Euler Frost edged his car back onto the main road. "It would still operate within certain narrow limits. Only the dangerous highs and lows would be eliminated from human activity. You can see how such a system would immediately benefit those of its backers who are industrialists. Take the electric auto, for instance. The computers would determine that buyers were returning to a cycle of red cars, and the manufacturers would turn out seventy percent of their cars in red. Buyers would have no choice but to conform to the prediction. Likewise hologram films and video cassettes and a million other products could be assured of maximum sales by marketing them in compliance with computer predictions."

"And the men behind this scheme?"

"Two of them—the two most prominent—are the ones whose names you found in that election computer. Jason Blunt and Stanley Ambrose. They have organized a company called Nova Industries as a front for their activities."

Earl Jazine nodded. "Now suppose you tell me how you know all this, and how you were on the scene to follow me tonight."

They had entered the traffic web leading back to Sunsite, and Euler Frost set his car on automatic control. He was not above letting the computers do some work for him on occasion. "Our people—the HAND people—have been onto this group for some time. Axman had developed the first leads before he got sent to prison, and I simply followed through. With the aid of an informer I learned that the group was planning their secret election one month ahead of the real one. They felt that with a shadow of government of sorts standing by, public acceptance of the real government's overthrow would be that much easier. Luckily, our informer was able to tell me the

50

location of the central election headquarters, and the fact that the candidates were Blunt and Ambrose."

"Has this secret election already been held?"

Euler Frost glanced at him, wondering just how much Jazine really knew about it. "I think so," he replied, "and I need to know who won. It makes a difference to our strategy whether the winner was Blunt or Ambrose. They're different men, with different goals. Axman never viewed Nova as a major threat, but I'm not making the same mistake."

"What do you need my help for?" Jazine asked.

"I have to get inside Nova's election headquarters to see the results. The place has fantastic electronic defenses that I can only begin to comprehend. I need an expert with computers and wiring mazes."

"Defenses didn't stop HAND at the Federal Medical Center," Jazine pointed out. "You just blasted your way through."

"It's not yet time for such a rash move. I want to see those election results without Blunt or Ambrose knowing I saw them."

"Why not wait until they tell their members the results? Then your informer can pass along the information."

"It may be too late by that time. My informer is very close to one of the candidates. If the other man won, I won't know anything in time to take countermeasures."

"If what you're telling me is true, I can get President McCurdy on the vision-phone and have these people arrested."

"No, for two reasons. There's not enough evidence of their plot, and such a move would only bring the government down on HAND again. I've served enough time in the Venus Colony."

That seemed to remind Jazine of something. "Did you know this Ambrose when you were there?"

"Only as a prisoner knows his warden."

"He wrote to his former mistress about you."

"How nice of him," Frost said dryly.

They drove for a time in silence, until finally Earl Jazine asked, "Just where is this secret election headquarters?"

"They have a building in Chicago. I could show you tomorrow."

Jazine grunted and was silent again.

6.
CARL CRADER

The first thing he noticed about the girl was her youthful beauty, and the lightness of her walk as she came forward to meet him on the dock. She shook his hand and introduced herself, and he was surprised to learn that this child was Jason Blunt's wife.

"You say he'll be back soon?" Carl Crader asked.

"Soon, yes. Won't you come in?"

She led the way up a landscaped path to a great cube of glass and metal that dominated the man-made drilling island. It was a house, he supposed, but such a house as he had never seen before. The door slid open silently as they approached, and closed just as gently behind them. She motioned to a great white couch that looked as if it might devour him, but Crader sank into it with surprising ease and found it really quite comfortable. The view through the front window, of the sea-rail line curving gently to the north, was truly breathtaking. It was obvious that the place was more of a home from the inside than it had appeared from the outside.

"Quite a place you have," Crader said. "Been here long?"

"Jason and I have been married three years. We

met in New Istanbul. I am Turkish."

"A credit to your country." He bowed a bit as he said it.

"Sometimes I miss New Istanbul," she confided. "Especially when Jason is away and I'm alone here. The house is fully automated, and we need only a few servants. They're very little company." She walked to the window and stared out at the sea. "Do you play aqua-golf, Mr. Crader?"

"I rarely have time."

"We have a nice little course here." She pointed out the window and he could see the familiar green pod anchored just off shore. Aqua-golf was the sport of a crowded civilization, where there was no longer space for the elaborate courses of the twentieth century. On little more than an acre of land, usually built over the water, this version of clock golf used a single grouping of holes at its center, with the eighteen courses laid out in a radiating pattern.

Crader heard the familiar roar of a descending rocketcopter and glanced skyward. "Would that be your husband?"

Masha nodded. "That would be him."

He followed her to the door to greet the trim, bearded man who bounded up the steps like a youth. Jason Blunt stopped short when he saw the visitor, and his questioning eyes were on Crader as he bent to kiss his wife.

"Darling, this is Carl Crader, from Washington."

"New York," Crader corrected. "Computer Investigation Bureau. Pleased to meet you, Mr. Blunt."

"You caught me at a busy time," Jason Blunt said. "As you can see, I've just returned . . ."

"Oh, I won't take up much of your time," Crader assured him, keeping it casual. "Just a few routine questions."

"Very well." He turned to his wife. "Masha, could you have some drinks mixed for us? We'll be in the solarium."

He led Crader down the hall to a large glassed-in room at the back of the house. It faced south, catching the maximum sunlight while presenting yet another panoramic view of the Gulf. Crader guessed the room to be fully thirty feet high, and even its ceiling was of glass, so that the whole effect was to stagger the visitor with a shimmering brilliance where light and water blended into one.

The room was almost devoid of furniture, though there were a few formfit lounges and a wireless vision-phone on a plastic stand. Jason Blunt slipped out of his jacket and stretched out on one of the lounges. Crader looked around, feeling uncomfortable, and finally chose to sit on the edge of the nearest lounge. "I won't take too much of your time," he repeated.

"I'd appreciate that."

Something about the line of his face as he relaxed brought back memories to Crader, and he asked, "Didn't you do some video acting in your younger days?"

Jason Blunt smiled at the recognition. "A touch of it. But my father never really approved. Acting today is such a feast for the makeup man, what with face foam and voice boxes. My father couldn't even recognize me on the video or the holograms, and thus he was against it from the beginning. Finally I gave it

55

up and joined him in his salvage work and the undersea oil drilling. That was nearly twenty years ago. I only wish he'd lived to see it now." His face clouded for a moment and then cleared. "But what brought you here, Mr. Crader?"

"Actually, it's about this election."

"McCurdy? Did he send you here for a contribution?"

"I meant the election between you and Ambrose."

Jason Blunt sat up. "I don't think I get your meaning."

"Well, I'll explain it, then. The FRIDAY-404 computer was secretly programmed to receive the results of an underground election of sorts between you and a man named Stanley Ambrose. A technician named Rogers discovered the programming in the FRIDAY unit before your people had a chance to erase it. He was later murdered, but not before we were called into the investigation. We think your opponent is the Stanley Ambrose who directed the Venus Colony."

That caused Blunt to stand. "You know a great deal. Do you have any proof of what you're saying?"

"Enough, and we're gathering more. You realize, sir, that a plot to overthrow our government . . ."

A chuckle here. "There is no plot! That's hogwash!"

"How would you describe it? A secret election is held, a man who discovers it is murdered, one of my own investigators is attacked . . ."

"Coincidence, nothing more." The overhead sun was reflecting off the polished floor at his feet, creating the impression of a man standing in a pool of

56

fire.

"But you admit the secret election was held? You admit to being a member of HAND?"

"HAND?" Jason Blunt roared with laughter. "I can assure you I have no connection whatsoever with that gang of criminals! The election certainly does not concern HAND!"

"Then what does it concern?"

He sighed and stroked his beard. "You realize, Crader, that you have no authority here. The Supreme Court ruled in 2020 that man-made drilling islands like this are beyond the jurisdiction of the USAC."

"I'm aware of the laws," Crader answered shortly.

Masha interrupted at that moment to serve drinks. "I hand-mix them for special guests," she said as Crader accepted his.

"Thanks. I appreciate it."

Jason Blunt took his drink and seemed to study the amber liquid. Then suddenly he came to a decision. "Stay here overnight, Crader. In the morning I'll fly you to Utah and tell you the whole story."

"Utah!"

"That's where it's at."

"Very well," Crader decided. "I'll take you up on it."

"Can I come along?" Masha asked.

Blunt seemed startled by his wife's request. He glanced at Crader and said, "Sure. Of course you can. It must get lonely for you here on the island. See what time dinner will be ready, and arrange one of the bedrooms for our guest. In the morning we fly to Utah."

57

Although the flight was nearly 1,500 miles long, Jason Blunt chose to make it in his private rocket-copter rather than transfer to a commercial jet at Houston airport. As a result, the trip lasted some three hours, most of which Carl Crader spent in the passenger compartment with Masha.

"Does he always sit up with the pilot?"

She shrugged. "Usually. I don't really travel with him that much. Occasional flights to New York, and that's about it. He has the yacht, of course, and I love that."

"How did you two happen to meet?"

She grinned a bit. "You wouldn't believe it if I told you."

"Try me."

"A friend introduced us. A man named Stevro, back in New Istanbul."

"You must have been very young."

"I was."

"They tell me Turkish girls are sometimes trained to wifely tasks and then sold to millionaire travelers. Is that true?"

"I wouldn't know," she said, blushing slightly.

"Have you ever been to this place in Utah before?"

"No. Never. Until recently, Jason never discussed business with me. Lately, with all the meetings . . ."

Blunt reappeared in the cabin, cutting short her sentence. "Well, Crader, it's hardly fair of you to be questioning my wife behind my back."

Crader started to deny the charge, but at his side Masha bristled. "It wasn't like that, Jason! We were

58

just talking!"

"I heard your talking, over the cabin speaker."

"You've started eavesdropping on me now?"

Blunt's face flushed with anger. "Remember what you are. Remember where I found you." He turned and reentered the pilot's cabin.

Embarrassed, Carl Crader watched the tears well in Masha's eyes. "The bastard! How . . . how can he be so nice sometimes and such a bastard other times?"

"Don't let it bother you," he said, trying to comfort her. His eyes were on the wall speaker, and he was certain Blunt was still monitoring their conversation.

She recovered a bit and stared out the window. "I'm all right," she said at last.

Crader decided to risk a renewal of Blunt's fury. "You mentioned meetings . . ."

"I'd better not talk about it," she said firmly.

"All right."

They lapsed into silence for the remainder of the flight, until Jason Blunt reappeared to announce they were coming down for a landing. He was pleasant and talkative, as if nothing had happened, and he pointed out the features of the landscape as they descended.

"Over there on your left is an old Indian reservation from the last century. And what we're landing on is a dry lake bed. There are lots of dry lakes in Utah. The whole damn state is a dry lake—or most of it, anyway. The northern section used to be part of the Great Salt Lake."

The copter touched down effortlessly. "There's

59

nothing here," Crader observed, scanning the horizon in all directions.

"Oh, there's something."

They stepped out of the rocketcopter and immediately the pilot reversed power to lift the machine off the desert floor. "He's leaving us!" Masha exclaimed, somewhat alarmed.

"We don't need him anymore right now." Jason Blunt produced a small electronic beeper from his pocket and pressed a coded signal. Almost at once a portion of the lake bed slid open as if by magic.

"What's this?" Crader asked.

"Follow me down. There's an elevator."

Crader and Masha followed along down the steel stairway to a little underground platform that faced blank doors. After a moment's wait the doors slid open soundlessly and they stepped into the elevator. "Amazing," Crader observed.

Jason Blunt smiled, pleased with the reaction. "I wish I could take credit for it, but this whole complex is government-built, left over from the missile hysteria of the last century. We are descending to a vast underground city that once housed missile defenses and the North American Air Defense command post. It was one of two such units. The other, in Wyoming, was demolished early in this century, but this survived—an amazing relic of twentieth-century man. One of my companies, Nova Industries, bought it from the government some years back. We told them we might use it for underground storage of natural gas, but as you'll see we have put it to another use."

The elevator ceased its descent, and the doors slid open. They walked down a long stainless steel corridor that reminded Crader of something seen in the old space films of the past. Through another door they encountered their first humans in the underground city—a dozen or so young men in white bodysuits who worked at computer consoles.

"Don't tell me this is all for the oil and natural gas business," Crader said. He'd seen vast computer complexes before, but nothing even approaching this.

"No, no. It's much more, really. In these memory banks are every fact, every statistic, every bit of historical information that goes to make up the United States of America and Canada." He moved to one of the vacant consoles. "I can summon up any figures, plot and trend, within seconds."

"They have something like this in Washington," Crader observed.

"Not like this! Two hundred men and women live in this underground city, working full time at the computers. Another five hundred come here occasionally, or communicate via terminals around the country. Here, let me show you the range of this thing."

He pressed a series of keys, watching the printout on the screen above the console. "Want to see a graph of federal highway expenditures over the past two hundred years?" Almost at once a steeply climbing line appeared on the screen, leveling off toward the top. "How about it, Crader? Ask it some questions. Go ahead! Anything!"

"All right," Crader said, accepting the challenge. "What was the Corliss Engine?"

Blunt's fingers flew over the console, and almost instantly the printout appeared: *"Colossal steam en-*

61

gine invented by George Henry Corliss and displayed at Philadelphia Centennial Exposition in 1876."

"Good?" Blunt asked.

"Good," Crader conceded.

"It plays games," Masha said. "All this for a machine that answers quiz questions?" She had the direct brashness of youth.

"It does much more than answer quiz questions," Blunt replied, a bit stiffly. "For instance, I can order up a chart of stock market cycles, or crime rates, or even revenue shares from legalized gambling. I can go further. Using the facts and figures of the past, I can predict the future with a high degree of accuracy."

"Who'll win next month's presidential election?" Crader asked.

"This is a projection on the popular vote." Blunt fed the question to the computer. The answer took four seconds:

ANDREW JACKSON MCCURDY 81,785,480
THOMAS PARK WALLACE 78,906,473

"Fairly close," Crader said. "Though as a department head I'm pleased to see that my boss will remain the same."

"I can break it down by state if you'd like."

"No need. What's your calculated margin of error?"

"Less than half of one percent."

"Very good. Now let's try this one. Who won the election between Jason Blunt and Stanley Ambrose?"

The bearded man merely smiled. "The computer will not have those figures. A unit in Chicago tabulates the results, and even I do not know what they

62

are."

He rose from the console and motioned them to follow. But the rest of the tour provided no new insights for Crader. There was only room after underground room of memory units and readout screens, with a brief glimpse of Blunt's office.

"Why?" he asked at last.

"Why?"

"If this is not part of some revolutionary scheme, then why?"

"This is not HAND, as you can see. Our group does not hate the machine. We know its capabilities, and we make use of them. Rather than destroy the machines, as HAND would do, we intend to harness them for the good of mankind. The idea of using computers to distill all of human knowledge is not new with us, of course. In the late 1960's *The New York Times* attempted something similar, feeding all indexed items from the *Times* into a central computer. A large series of books and research projects resulted—everything from a directory and index of all the films ever shown in New York to an alphabetical listing of all the people whose deaths the *Times* had reported. Way back then there were those who voiced objections to the project, pointing out that the computer input could tend to color or distort the true facts of a more detailed news story. But the project was successful nonetheless. Here we have simply carried it one step further. We record the past, and use it to define the present while predicting the future."

"If that's true, you could rule the country with this machine. Rule it better than the President."

"Perhaps," Blunt said, smiling slightly.

"Then you admit your group could function as a sort of secret super-government?"

"Oh, certainly. I admit to everything. You must only trust me that our intentions are honorable. The very fact I brought you here shows our intentions are honorable."

"What about Stanley Ambrose's intentions?"

"Ambrose?"

"Obviously there are two factions fighting for control here. Otherwise, why hold a secret election? If Ambrose won that election, what happens?"

"Ambrose is an honorable man, a dedicated public servant."

"He's not been seen since his return from Venus a year ago. Any idea where he is?"

"He has been here many times. Soon I'm sure he'll return to public view."

They'd come back to the stainless steel corridor leading to the elevators. "We've seen it all," Blunt said, "except for the crew's living quarters."

"Crew? As on a spaceship?"

"It's very like a spaceship, isn't it?"

"It's cut off from reality with no view of earth, if that's what you mean."

"Will you report us to the President?"

Crader weighed the man's words, wondering if they would be followed by a threat. "Of course," he answered finally. "It's my job. Am I free to leave?"

"Certainly! You were never a prisoner." He waved his hand. "Report what you like. We have no secrets."

"Then why did the rocketcopter leave so quickly after it deposited us? I had the distinct impression you were trying to avoid having our location pinpointed by anyone who might be following."

A shrug. "A simple precaution against HAND. We remember what they did at the Federal Medical Center."

"All right," Crader said. "You showed me all this, and you showed it for a reason. You want me to carry a message back to President McCurdy."

"That is correct."

"What message?"

"Tell him what you saw here. Tell him . . ." Jason Blunt paused, choosing his words with care. "Tell him the future belongs to those with the largest computers."

7.
EARL JAZINE

He'd been in Chicago only once in the last decade, on a routine computer investigation involving fraudulent tax returns. The city had changed little in the meantime, though it still reminded Jazine of a compact New York, throwing its towers to the sky but never quite equaling the lure of Manhattan.

He'd left Euler Frost at the jetport, and while Frost scouted the location of the secret election headquarters, Jazine used the time to have photo prints made of the material in his microfilm camera. He read again the Venus letter of Stanley Ambrose, and saw again the man's smiling face at his softball game.

"Stanley Ambrose, where are you?"

No answer came, because there was no one in the hotel room to answer him. He sighed and flipped on the vision-phone, punching out the direct line to Carl Crader's office at CIB headquarters. When he saw Judy on the other end, he said, "Hi, doll! The chief around?"

"No, and I'm beginning to worry. He hadn't planned to be away overnight."

"Have you checked with Jason Blunt?"

66

"Not yet, but I may have to. How about you, Earl? Where are you?"

"Chicago. With Euler Frost."

"Frost!"

"It's a long story. Look, I should be back by tomorrow. If the chief shows up, tell him." He blew her a kiss and clicked off. Frost should be calling soon, and he wanted the phone to be free.

Jazine met Euler Frost toward evening, in the area of downtown once referred to as the Loop. They traveled along a moving sidewalk until they reached a tall, slender building near the lakefront.

"This is the place," Frost explained. "Nova Industries. All we have to do is get in."

"Shouldn't be too difficult," Jazine said. "Just stick with me."

Nova Industries occupied the entire seventy-sixth floor of the building, and they quickly established that the elevator was programmed to bypass that floor after six o'clock. Since newer buildings like this lacked fire stairs, Jazine knew there was no other way onto the floor. "It's like a time lock on a bank vault," he explained to Frost. "But there is a way to beat it."

"How?"

Jazine worked quickly inside the elevator, flipping a panel to expose the clockwork mechanism. From his pocket he produced a miniature electromagnet which he pressed against the face of the clock. "These new time locks are great, but you can speed them up if you know how." He started to rotate the electromagnet. "This'll be the fastest night this eleva-

67

tor ever saw!"

He took the magnet away and pressed the button for the seventy-sixth floor. Nothing happened. He tried again, advancing the clock another hour. This time when he pressed the button the number 76 lit up. "We're on our way," he said softly to Euler Frost.

The offices of Nova Industries were like a dozen others Earl Jazine had checked out during the past year. A dummy corporation always operated along certain standard lines, whether its purpose was the changing of race-track odds or the overthrow of the federal government.

"Computer terminals," Frost said, shining his light around.

"You don't need that thing." Jazine adjusted the polarized windows and flipped on the radiant ceiling. "Now you take those files while I check out these computers."

It was long, tiring work, but at the end of an hour he had what they'd come for. The election figures had been erased from the FRIDAY-404 system by the man who killed Rogers, so it was necessary for Jazine to counterfeit a signal to the master memory unit to obtain the data he needed. It was something like an old-fashioned safe cracker testing the combinations of the vault.

Finally, though, he had it. Over 80,000 votes had been cast in the election, which took place on October 1st. They had come from the USAC mainly, but there was scattered overseas voting from various Nova subsidiaries and drilling islands. The result was the same as the figures Jazine had first discovered in

68

the FRIDAY-404 system, but he didn't tell Frost.

STANLEY AMBROSE   45,390

JASON BLUNT   36,455

They left the Nova offices the same way they'd entered, and Jazine set back the time clocks with his electromagnet. Then they returned to his hotel room and looked over what they had.

"The election has been held, and it appears that Ambrose won." Euler Frost bit his lip and frowned. "It doesn't help me or my informant at all."

"If you could tell me who your informant is . . ."

"A young lady very close to Jason Blunt."

"His wife?"

"I can't tell you any more. I've told you too much already." He picked up the little plastic overnight case he carried and started to open it. "Earl, I have to ask you to help me on something else."

"I've bent the rules already," Jazine said. "I don't know how far I can go without reporting to the chief. What is it now?"

"There are many people affiliated with HAND throughout the world. They are Graham Axman's people mainly, since he did much of the organizing for HAND while I was a political prisoner on the Venus Colony."

"We'd like to have a list of those people."

"So you could arrest them? Ship them all off to Venus? Can't you see that the Blunt—Ambrose group, whatever it is, represents a far greater threat to this country than HAND? They are organized enough to hold secret elections, using the regular equipment for a presidential election. The figures we found indicate this group has over eighty thousand voting members! Can you imagine what a secret society of eighty thousand members could do to this country?"

"Not much," Jazine observed. "In the last century there were plenty of pressure groups with more members than that—a few even bent on revolution—and they never got anywhere."

"But they didn't have computers, did they?" Frost asked triumphantly. "No, if HAND stands aside and lets them win this one . . ."

"Just what do you intend doing?"

"That's the point! I've kept HAND going in this country, but without Axman I'm helpless on the overseas contacts. That island in the Indian Ocean, those Oriental girls he used so well . . ."

"Why do you need me?"

"I need you because I need Graham Axman. HAND needs Graham Axman."

"He's in prison," Jazine said, stating the obvious.

"In prison and due for transfer to the Venus Colony."

"I don't know about that."

"Well, I do! His lawyer told me last week! Earl, I've been to the Venus Colony. I know what it's like up there."

"I thought Ambrose did away with the penal aspects while he was there."

"I'm the living proof that he didn't! The Venus Colony has become our Siberia. Instead of sending families there like the Russo-Chinese do, we deport criminals and political prisoners."

"Axman broke the law. You're damned lucky you're not in prison with him."

Euler Frost stood there, weighing his next words. Finally he spoke. "We have to get him out, Earl."

70

"Out?"

"Out of prison. You have to help me get him out, like you helped me tonight."

"Hey, wait a minute! That business tonight was one thing, but helping a federal prisoner to escape is something else! You seem to forget whose side I'm on!"

"I was hoping you were on HAND's side."

"Well, I'm not. I could arrest you for just talking about helping Axman escape. The only reason I've gone along with you this far is because you saved my life in that damned salt mine!"

"Since you owe me a life, give me Graham Axman's."

Earl Jazine shook his head. "It's not mine to give."

Frost looked almost sad. "Very well," he said, "then I'll do it without you."

"I may have to prevent that."

Jazine moved forward, around the bed, as Euler Frost's hand came out of his bag. He was holding a stunner. "I'm sorry about this."

"Hell," Jazine barked, "not twice in one week!" He launched himself across the bed at Frost, and he was half in the air when the stunner caught him in the side. He felt the thud of the concussion against his body, felt the instant of pain on his already broken ribs, and went down hard.

When he came to, a half hour later, Euler Frost was gone. He established that fact and then simply stayed where he was on the floor. For a long time he was afraid to move his body, afraid of feeling the stab of pain in his broken ribs. Finally, after another

71

quarter hour, he slowly propped himself up on one arm and used the bed to pull himself up the rest of the way. He felt like hell, but no further damage seemed to have been done to his ribs.

He started to phone New York, and then realized the office would be closed now. The best thing he could do would be to warn the prison where Axman was being held, and then hop the next jetliner back home. He placed a call to the warden at the Federal Correctional Institute in Kansas City. The deputy warden was on duty at that hour, and his face on the vision-phone screen was bored and disinterested. He noted the information and promised Jazine that no one would be escaping from his prison that night or any other night.

Feeling that he'd done all he could, Jazine checked out of the hotel and flew back to New York.

The next day was Friday, and he found Carl Crader in the office quite early, running over some reports with Sabin and a new man from the commerce unit. Jazine chatted with Judy until he was free, and then ran rapidly through his experiences since leaving the hospital.

Crader listened in silence, and only spoke at the end. "Do you have the pictures?"

"Pictures?" Jazine had almost forgotten about them. "Oh, sure—you mean of Stanley Ambrose and his letter to Milly Norris."

Crader took the prints and spread them out on his desk. He seemed to be searching for something, but Jazine couldn't imagine what. Finally he said, "I don't know. I just don't know."

72

"What, chief?"

"Much of what you've told me jibes with my own experiences with Jason Blunt. He admitted the existence of a secret organization, and even admitted the election part of it. He flew me to Utah to inspect an underground computer complex that would make your mouth water. But the way Blunt tells it, his group is a benefit to the nation, not a threat."

"Was it a benefit when they kidnapped me and tried to kill me in that salt mine?"

"That's just the trouble," Crader said.

"What trouble?"

"These pictures."

"What about them?" Jazine walked to the desk and peered down at the prints.

"Well, you had the camera in your pocket when you were imprisoned in the radioactive salt mine, right?"

"Yes, but . . ."

"Earl, if that salt mine had been radioactive, it would have fogged the film in your camera. Since the prints show no fogging, it means there was no radioactivity. You were never in danger in that salt mine. Euler Frost rescued you from nothing at all. The whole kidnapping and rescue was an elaborate HAND plot."

8.

CARL CRADER

Jazine sat down. "I can't believe it, chief."

"The facts speak for themselves, Earl. Euler Frost lied about following you there. He lied about rescuing you. If you stop to think about it, why should these masked men kidnap you, drive you an hour away, talk about a trial, and then send you down the chute into a salt mine? It sounds more like one of those old lodge initiations than a serious attempt at murder. True assassins would have finished the job when they had you naked in that woman's bed."

"I knew I shouldn't have told you that part!" Jazine complained.

"He used you, Earl. Frost used you."

"For what?"

"To get into that Chicago office building. And to spring Axman from jail. When he saw you wouldn't go that far, he used his stunner on you."

"Yeah."

"What I don't know is where that leaves us. Since Frost lied to you about one thing, did he lie to you about everything? Did I get the straight story from Jason Blunt after all?"

"What about the attack on me at the zooitorium?

74

That was no joke!"

"True enough. Nor was the murder of Rogers. But which side is the tattooed man on?" Crader thought for a moment and then answered his own question. "Not HAND's, certainly, because if they were so anxious to kill you a few days ago, they'd have finished the job when they had you a prisoner."

"All right," Jazine agreed. "So what do we do now?"

"Report to President McCurdy," Carl Crader said promptly. "As yet he knows nothing about this secret election business, nor does he know about Jason Blunt's underground computer complex. I also have something of a message for him, from Blunt."

"The President's not going to like it," Jazine predicted.

"You don't have to tell me that."

"He's especially not going to like all this tampering with the FRIDAY-404 computer, just four weeks before election day."

Crader knew that Earl had a good point. President McCurdy, running for reelection against the former governor of Ontario, would be concerned that the affair might raise questions about the accuracy of the computerized tally. "All right, Earl, let's tackle that problem before it even arises. Can you get Lawrence Friday to fly to Washington with us this afternoon and help reassure the President?"

"I can get him if he's willing to leave his animals." Jazine reached for the vision-phone. "But this time I'll try calling him. No more trips to the zooitorium for me!"

"Ask him to be here at one. We'll take the rocket-

75

copter down. With luck he'll be back by four."

"Right."

Crader buzzed for Judy. "Phone the New White House, Judy. Try to clear a one thirty appointment with the President for myself, Earl, and Lawrence Friday. Tell them it's urgent."

Crader had never met Lawrence Friday before, though he recognized the slender, stoop-shouldered man at once from his holograms. "Sorry to take you away from your animals," he said by way of greeting.

"No, no." Friday waved away the apology. "It was a slow day anyway. And one doesn't get a summons to the New White House every day."

The flight from the top of the World Trade Center to the copter pad at the New White House took just twenty-five minutes, which was good time. They were kept waiting only a few moments before being ushered down the sterile steel corridors to the presidential lounge. Though the bombproof nature of the building had been necessitated by the bombing of the original White House in 2018, the metal walls still reminded Crader unpleasantly of Jason Blunt's underground city.

President Andrew Jackson McCurdy was a man of the people. Like his famous namesake two centuries earlier, he ruled the party with an iron fist and was a vigorous spokesman for the wishes of the voters. And yet, for all of that, there was something almost wise and fatherly about President McCurdy. He had just enough gray in his hair to contrast sharply with the string of boyish chief executives who'd preceeded him, just enough fire in his speech to excite the voters one more time.

"How are you, Carl?" he asked, stepping forward to greet them. "Good to see you again. And Earl . . . And Professor Friday, I believe. I've been an admirer of your work for some time."

"Thank you, sir," Friday replied.

"I hope you're going to get me reelected next month!"

"I hope so too. The FRIDAY-404 is ready for those returns!"

"Good, good. Now, Carl—just what was so urgent?"

They sat down and Crader began. "You aren't going to like this, sir."

"Try me."

"The FRIDAY-404 system has been used by a private group to hold some sort of election. The balloting took place last week—on October first—involving upwards of eighty thousand persons throughout the USAC and overseas."

"What? What are you talking about, Carl?"

"A secret election."

"For what?"

"Possibly for a shadow government to replace the legal government of the USAC."

"But how could such a thing be? How could they gain access to the system?"

"They didn't gain access to each individual voting machine, of course, but they did manage to tie into the regional relay stations, and through them to the orbiting satellite we use. The data on the secret election apparently was then fed back to earth to their

77

own computers. A random signal managed to reach the FRIDAY system, though, and it was discovered before it could be erased. That's how we found out about it."

President McCurdy scratched his nose. It was obvious he still didn't believe a word of it. "Who were the candidates in this so-called election?"

"Jason Blunt, the millionaire oilman, and Stanley Ambrose, former director of the Venus Colony."

"Ambrose! I wouldn't put anything past Jason Blunt—but Ambrose! Does he admit his part in this?"

"We haven't been able to locate him, sir. He seems to have disappeared since returning from Venus last year."

"Disappeared?" The President pondered that. "And what about Jason Blunt?"

"He admits the existence of this group, but claims there is no intention to overthrow the government. He took me on a tour of an underground computer complex in Utah." Crader described the place in detail.

"I'll find out who sold that site to them, you can be damn sure!"

"I understand it was disposed of as surplus government property, purchased by one of Blunt's firms for the underground storage of natural gas."

"We'll see about that." McCurdy puzzled over it a moment and then asked, "If their computer complex is as big as you say, why did they need to tie into the FRIDAY system for their secret election?"

"Perhaps only to show us the extent of their power," Crader surmised, but he wasn't fully satis-

78

fied with that explanation.

"Anything else?"

"Blunt sent you a message. He said the future belongs to those with the largest computers."

"Sounds like a threat to me," McCurdy said after a moment's thought.

"Perhaps," Crader conceded.

"I know Blunt. He backed my opponent four years ago."

"Is he backing Thomas Wallace this time?"

"Not that I know of. Until your news I thought he was sitting this election out."

"His computers predict a narrow victory for you next month."

"That's generous of him!" President McCurdy snorted. Then, perhaps remembering that Friday was present, he shifted to a more statesmanlike attitude. "But tell me, Professor Friday, is there any possibility that this tampering with your election computer could affect the results of next month's contest?"

It was the question Crader had known would be asked, and the professor was ready. "There's nothing to worry about, sir. As with any type of computer, the magnetic tapes and memory cells can be cleared through a simple operation. It won't interfere with the election in any way."

But the President was far from satisfied. "Nevertheless, doesn't the very ease with which these interlopers gained access to the FRIDAY-404 system cast a cloud over it? Suppose I should win the election next month by a few million votes, and suppose my opponent then suggests that the computer system was tampered with, through the unauthorized insertion of fraudulent votes? He could point to this happening to bolster his case."

Lawrence Friday shook his head. "The two events are entirely different. In this case last week, the unguarded voting machines and computer circuits were used to relay results of a private election to a central office in Chicago. Next month's voting will be entirely different. There'll be the usual poll watchers, plus continuous monitoring of the skysphere satellite and a constant check of the readouts. The votes are cast at a predictable rate, depending upon the hour of the day and the number of states having open polls. If, say, there was a sudden surge of three million votes within a minute around two o'clock, we'd know something was wrong because not that many people vote at midday. Likewise, if any fraudulent votes were fed into the system a few at a time we'd discover it too, because the running totals for the candidates are constantly checked against the votes cast all around the country. Your votes plus Thomas Wallace's votes have to equal the total votes cast, and there's no possibility of cheating."

"You explain it very well," President McCurdy said, somewhat relieved.

Friday hurried on to offer more reassuring details, and at the end of another half hour the President was satisfied. He got to his feet and shook hands all around. "Carl, I hope you'll keep on this matter involving Jason Blunt. I've never had any great admiration for the man, and I wouldn't be surprised at anything he attempted."

"We're continuing our investigation, sir. Earl and I are handling it personally. We're also checking any possible involvement by HAND."

"HAND! I thought their leader was in prison!"

"He is, but there are some others still around."

McCurdy shook his head. "Bad business. We can't afford to have them blowing up computers so close to election." He got to his feet. "Carry on, gentlemen. I know the matter is in good hands."

He disappeared through a rear door and they were ushered back into the metal-walled corridor. "It seemed to go well," Friday observed.

Carl Crader nodded. "As well as could be expected, I suppose. He was a bit disturbed toward the end when I mentioned HAND, though."

"Is HAND a real danger?" Friday asked.

"It could be. They were a danger just last year, and some of their important members are still at large." Crader didn't bother to add that he'd once had Euler Frost in his grasp and allowed him to escape. That was another story, but the affair had left him with a certain degree of respect for Frost.

The rocketcopter was waiting on its pad for the flight back to New York. They dropped Professor Friday in Central Park near the zooitorium and then flew on to the top of the World Trade Center.

"Earl, you said you checked the prison where Graham Axman is being held?"

"That's right. If they let Axman escape now, it's not our fault."

Crader nodded and went back to his desk to check on the accumulation of messages that always awaited him. There seemed nothing else to be done on the Blunt—Ambrose matter, at least not for the moment.

9.
EULER FROST

He had not wanted to use the stunner on Earl Jazine. The girl he loved had been killed by such a weapon on Venus, and he knew of too many other serious injuries caused by the concussion gun. But at its lowest setting he gambled it would be safe. When Jazine had tried to jump him there'd been little choice, after all, and the weapon had been ready.

He'd built up his plan to enlist Jazine's aid over a period of several weeks, and when he learned the CIB man was in Sunsite to question Milly Norris it was an opportunity that couldn't be overlooked. If it hadn't worked out completely as planned, at least Jazine had helped him at the Nova office—something he might not have accomplished on his own. He only wished there'd been time to leave a calling card at Nova, in the form of a hydrobomb like they'd used on the Federal Medical Center computers.

But now Jazine was gone from his plans, and Graham Axman still waited behind bars. Axman's trial following the bombing of the computers had been swift and efficient. He and two lesser HAND members had drawn twenty-year sentences, and that was the end of it. A few telenewspapers applauded

82

the verdicts, pointing out the danger of any group opposed to the machine-dominated culture, but most had simply remained silent. The affair had passed quickly from the front pages, and to most people Graham Axman and HAND were only half-remembered disturbances in a constantly changing world.

Euler Frost had spent the previous month scouting the area around the Federal Correctional Institute at Kansas City. The prison, opened in 2011 to replace the outmoded facilities at nearby Leavenworth, was a model of twenty-first-century penology. It was a low, sprawling structure with unbreakable plastic windows instead of bars, fully air-conditioned, and with a hologram screen and telenews printer in every cell. The prisoners spent four hours a day attending classes, and four hours working at a trade. Progressive and comfortable as it was, the prison was also escapeproof. Each cell was equipped with a proximity scanner to check on the inmate's presence day or night. The walls were guarded by a screen of laser beams that crisscrossed the courtyard, and every vehicle leaving the prison grounds was X-rayed for stowaways.

Euler Frost learned all this and was not discouraged.

When he'd first come from the Venus Colony prison last year, Graham Axman had taken him in, helped him find a new life, even transported him to HAND's island headquarters at Plenish in the Indian Ocean. All this was what Frost remembered, and he knew he could not allow Axman to remain in prison for the better part of twenty years. He knew also that if the government made good its threat of exile to the

Venus Colony, Axman would be beyond the help of him or anyone else.

If escape from the Federal Correctional Institute was impossible, then Frost would just have to see that Axman escaped from outside the prison.

The talk of shifting the HAND leader to Venus began to play an important part in the emerging escape plan. It was an easy job to determine that official messages were sent to the prison via a closed-circuit teleprinter from Washington. Frost had wanted Earl Jazine to send a false message to the prison, bouncing it off the comsat satellite. Now that was something Frost would have to do himself.

On Saturday morning he put his plan into effect, summoning Sam Venray, the black man who'd been at his side during the attack on the medical center, and who had worn one of the masks when they kidnapped Jazine. Venray was a small but agile man, with quick, white eyes accented by the blackness of his skin. In an era when mass intermarriage had all but ended the race problem, Venray held himself aloof, refusing even to date a white woman. Frost had asked him once what he was hoping to accomplish and Venray only replied, "I want to keep the blackness in." It was to keep the blackness in, somehow, that he had joined HAND. "Humans Against Neuter Domination—yeah, man, that sounds like me!"

Now, facing him in a Kansas City hotel room, Frost said, "Sam, I want you to get out there and watch the prison. Rent an electric and drive up and down by the main gate if you have to. My message will request that Axman be moved from the prison to the Kansas City jetport for transportation to Washington and then to the Venus Colony."

"You sure they'll move him today?"

"I'm requesting it."

"They'll check back with Washington to confirm," the black man pointed out quite logically.

"That's why I picked a Saturday. There'll be no one in the Washington office to confirm or deny, and I'm betting they'll go ahead with the transfer. They've already received preliminary word of it, so the news won't be any big surprise."

"So, I'm watching the main gate. Then what?"

"They'll bring him out in a prison van. That's where we have to gamble a bit. We can't be sure he'll be inside, but we'll have to chance it." Frost unrolled a dimension map. "This is the shortest route to the airport. You follow along. A couple of the boys will be waiting here to laser the tires. I'll be above, in a rocketcopter, to handle the rest."

"What if they kill him?"

Euler Frost shrugged. "It would be better than twenty years on Venus, believe me."

The message was sent at noon, and one hour later Frost was riding above Kansas City at the controls of the rocketcopter. He watched the lines of electric cars on the expressways below, headed for the countryside and the nearby man-made lakes on one of the last warm weekends of autumn. Climate Control had predicted sunshine and there was plenty of it, reflecting off the cockpit window with such dazzling effect that Frost had to turn up the polarization.

For the first two hours nothing happened, and he

was beginning to sense failure in the air. Surely the prison director had decided to wait till Monday, when a check with Washington could be made. Surely he sensed something wrong.

Then, at a few minutes after three o'clock, the radio crackled into life. Sam Venray's voice came to him. "Prison van just pulling out. This looks like it."

"Hang in there, Sam. Any sign of extra guards?"

"Negative."

"Where are they? I can't see them yet."

"Van just cleared the laser beams. Heading north on the expressway."

"Right! Got it!" Frost signaled to the men in the cockpit with him and dropped the rocketcopter a thousand feet straight down.

That was when he saw the second van leaving the prison gates.

"Damn!"

"What is it?" the copilot asked.

But Frost was busy rousing Venray on his pocket radio. "Sam, there's a second van! About a mile behind you!"

"Oh, oh! That's bad news. Think they're wise?"

"Maybe. At least they're taking no chances."

"What now?"

"Proceed as planned, and let's see what happens."

He dropped a bit lower and saw the glint of the laser beam shoot out from the roadside. The first prison van blew all four tires at once and came to a sudden halt. Armored tires were fine against bullets, but a laser got to them every time.

Frost saw the smoke bombs hit and dropped lower for the kill. But his eyes were focused down the road,

86

to see what the second prison van would do. Almost at once it headed for an expressway down-ramp, apparently warned by radio of the trouble ahead. He debated only an instant before going after it. If one of the vans was a decoy, it could only be the first one. There was no point in sending the decoy along later.

He fired both rear rockets to put him ahead of the van, and then banked sharply to come down in front of it. "Get the tires," he told the man at his side.

"You're sure he's in there?"

"I'm sure."

The laser gun hit the front tires and brought the electric van to a sudden halt. Frost released a pair of smoke rockets as they landed and opened the hatch on his side. He was the first one out, running ahead of the others, using night goggles to see through the blinding smoke that already covered the roadway.

The door on the side of the van slid open, revealing a uniformed guard with a laser gun. Frost gave him a quick shot with the stunner and pushed his body out of the way, climbing into the van before the driver could react. He hated to use the stunner in the close confines of the van, but there was no other way. The driver's head bounced back against the plastic window as the shock wave hit him.

Then Frost pulled the release on the dashboard, opening the rear door. The others from the rocket-copter had reached the van by now, and he heard them in the back, heard a scream and the familiar crackle of a laser gun. He hopped back out of the van in time to see Sam Venray bending over a fallen guard.

"Did you need to kill him?" Frost barked.

"No choice," Venray said.

"Is Graham in there?"

"Here!" a familiar voice shouted, and Graham Axman emerged from the prison van, his legs hobbled by chains, his hands fighting the smoke from his eyes.

Frost grabbed him by the shoulder. "Just hang onto me, Graham. Here, Sam—use that laser on the leg irons. Come on now, Graham. The rocketcopter is down the road about a hundred feet. Put these goggles on so you can see."

Graham Axman ran along at his side, and he did not speak again until they were safely in the rocketcopter. "This is a damn sight better than a trip to Venus!" he said then.

"I thought you'd like it," Euler Frost replied with a smile. "Good to have you back again."

Graham Axman had lost weight during his months in confinement. His eyes still held the same fire, but without his familiar pointed beard there was less of the Satanic about him. Although he was still in his early forties, prison had aged and weakened him. The transformation was shocking to Frost at first, because he had never dreamed that anything could blunt the vigor of the man.

"I'll be all right," Axman said in response to his concern. "Give me a few days, that's all. They feed you tranquilizers in prison, in the coffee, and it takes a few days for the stuff to wear off."

But as the days of early October wore on and Axman's beard began to grow again, he still had not recovered his full vigor. Talking with him three days after the escape in their hiding place at a deserted farm, Frost found him interested in HAND, but only in a remote, scholarly way. "Tell me what you have been doing," he urged Frost. "Let me see how well I instructed you."

"Well enough for me to free you," Frost reminded him.

"What was it you said earlier about the Computer Cops?"

"I nearly tricked one of them into helping me free you. His name is Earl Jazine, and he works very close to Carl Crader. I arranged his kidnapping in such a manner that it would appear the work of the Nova group. Then I appeared on the scene to rescue him, in order to win his help. It worked to some extent, and he did assist me in entering the Nova offices in Chicago, but when I suggested he might help me free you, he balked."

"Nova, Nova! You mention them often, Euler, but I am not convinced of their danger."

"Believe me, Graham, much has happened during the months of your imprisonment."

"Certainly! You have taken over the leadership of HAND!"

For the first time Frost caught the harshness of his tone, the bitterness of his words. "Not at all," he said hurriedly. "Someone was needed to hold the group together until your release. That is all I have done."

"And Nova?"

"Nova is a menace, Graham. Their memory banks hold the very life and heritage of this nation, the soul of the land. Nova proposes to use a knowledge of the past to perpetuate that past. They desire a machine-controlled society where any sort of revolutionary change would be impossible."

But Graham Axman merely shook his head. "The real enemy is still in Washington, Euler, and you must never forget it! The machines of the government are what control us and stifle us. The people will never be really free until President McCurdy is gone."

Frost frowned at the words. "That doesn't sound like you, Graham. It's not a man HAND's been fighting all these years—it's a system."

"A man put me in prison. A man wanted me shipped to Venus."

But Frost shook his head. "McCurdy is not the enemy. Not the main enemy, at least. Nova has held a secret election to name the president of their revolutionary state. The man we must destroy is Stanley Ambrose, and after him Jason Blunt. With Blunt and Ambrose removed, Nova will be leaderless."

Axman's eyes sparkled with fire. "Not Nova. First President McCurdy, and then we will see. With HAND in charge, Nova will merely wither away."

"Graham . . ."

"I had much time to think in prison, Euler. HAND must be reorganized from top to bottom. I am once more taking command, but this time of a new and rejuvenated group. Even the name will change, Euler. From now on we will be the Fellowship of the HAND."

"Fellowship?" Frost was reminded of Tolkien's century-old novel, *The Fellowship of the Ring,* and Edgar Wallace's even older book, *The Fellowship of*

90

the Frog. He'd read them both in his youth, when children still read books, and he remembered Wallace's criminals taking orders from a mysterious voice that issued from the statue of a frog. "Doesn't that sound a bit juvenile?"

Graham Axman sighed and stretched out his slim fingers. "Euler, do you remember how we met in Paris when you were only sixteen and still mourning the death of your father? Do you remember how I took you by sea-rail to Plenish, in the Indian Ocean? Do you remember those early days when our organization was nameless, leaderless, almost purposeless? And do you remember how you came back to me in Washington last year, and how we worked together to strike our first blow at the machines?"

"I remember," Frost said softly.

"In those days it did not seem so juvenile, did it? In those days you were willing to follow where I led."

"You forget one thing, Graham. I served ten years of my life in prison, much of it on Venus, for my part in the organization."

"And I only served a few months?" The tone was mocking, scornful.

"I've earned the right, Graham. I'm not taking over your leadership of HAND, but I've earned the right to have my opinions respected."

"And your opinions are . . . ?"

"Call it what you will—HAND must face its real enemy. And that enemy is not in the New White House but in the underground computer complex of Nova Industries."

Axman tugged at the bristles on his chin. Finally he said simply, "We will talk of this another time."

10.

GRAHAM AXMAN

He had lived his life as a bitter man, one who watched humanity slip away to be replaced by the megamachine, the god of technology. His own boyhood had not been all that different from Euler Frost's, though he had lived it in the exotic East. Much of his time had been spent on the man-made island of Plenish, constructed as a tourist resort in the early twenty-first century by a pair of Greek billionaires.

His father was the entertainment director on the island, staging theatrical events in the ultramodern theater where the wealthy could relax after a day of aqua-golf or an evening of gambling. Young Graham learned much during those days in the theater. He learned the rudiments of acting, and once disguised himself as a minister to travel by sea-rail with Carl Crader, luring him into a trap on Plenish.

But he'd learned other things as well among the scrims and flats of backstage life. Like most theater in the early days of the twenty-first century, his father's productions were of a highly charged sexual nature. They were the type of shows the wealthy wanted to see in their leisure time, much as the

92

nobles of ancient Rome must have found a sexual outlet at the amphitheater.

Young Graham's sexual initiation had come at the hands of a tall Chinese woman in his father's theatrical company. Twice each night she was realistically ravaged onstage to the bleeping of electronic music controlled by her brain waves. At the moment of orgasm the music reached its peak, and members of the audience had been known to join in at this point until the theater sometimes resembled an orgy scene from some hologram by Watts.

The Chinese woman, whose name he could not now recall, had died one night when a sudden surge of electronic feedback pulverized her brain cells. Graham Axman had been saddened by the tragedy, and for a time his father's theater remained closed. Then, when he tried to reopen it, tragedy struck again. The exact nature of it had never been known to Graham. A machine had killed his father, they said. One of the machines onstage. The same one that killed the woman? He never knew, and nobody ever told him.

His mother had vanished somewhere into the resorts of Easter Island a decade earlier, and might be there still, relaxing beneath a solar mirror for all he knew. He did not venture to Easter Island to find out, nor did he remain on the island of Plenish. He went instead to Paris, where he took a job as a binary assistant and began to nurture his growing hatred of the machine.

It was in Paris some years later that he met young Euler Frost and returned with him to the island of Plenish. In the meantime Axman had lived through a succession of stormy love affairs, perhaps seeking the unattainable Chinese woman to replace that which he'd lost. He never found her, but her place was taken in turn by a wealthy English girl who taught him a catalog of standard perversions, a French prostitute who introduced him to the delights of the electric lance, and finally by an uninhibited Swedish boy.

Graham Axman was only beginning to come to grips with his bisexual nature at the time of his meeting with Euler Frost. That first summer together on Plenish, he'd been quickly rebuffed by Frost when he attempted intimacies. He had not tried it again, but his attitude toward the boy had been shaped and hardened by that moment in the sun.

Later, when Euler Frost was imprisoned for his part in their still nameless organization, Axman put him out of mind. He began building HAND, recruiting men like Sam Venray. Malcontents, mainly—men who would oppose the system because Graham Axman promised a better life somewhere in the foggy future.

He was startled when Frost made good his escape from a Venus Colony and returned to earth, but he was ready to harness the young man's hatreds to his own use. They'd gone back to Plenish once more, and while Frost dallied with a Chinese girl, Graham Axman was busy gathering his strike force for HAND's first mission.

Now, nearly a year later, Axman was gathering them again. Only two others had been arrested with him, and they were easily replaced. Venray was there to help him, though even the agile black man was developing a liking for Frost that Axman mistrusted.

"How many do we have?" he asked Venray one

94

morning a week after his escape.

"Sixteen right now."

"Have we contacted all the old ones?"

"Euler kept track of them."

"I didn't ask what Euler did! Have we contacted them?"

"Yes." The black man seemed embarrassed.

"And we only have sixteen? We had twelve on the Chin-Chan team for the attack on the Federal Medical Center."

"Some have scattered. We have the people back on Plenish, of course, but any movement of them would excite government suspicion."

"All right," Axman agreed finally. "We can do it with sixteen."

Venray stared down at his feet. "You're planning to attack the New White House?"

"I am."

"Euler doesn't think that's a good idea."

"Fuck Euler! You take orders from me!"

"Yes."

"Understood?"

"Yes."

"Very well. Assemble them. We'll have a planning session tomorrow morning."

Euler Frost came to him in the morning, just before the meeting. "I have someone special I'd like you to meet, Graham. Someone who's helped us a great deal."

"Who would that be?"

"A young woman named Mildred Norris. She was once an intimate of Stanley Ambrose, and she helped

95

me trap Earl Jazine."

"Bring her in."

The woman who entered the room was slim and pretty, with dark eyes and dyed blue hair. Axman let his gaze wander up the length of her legs, outlined by a black bodysuit. "Mildred Norris?"

"Everyone calls me Milly," she said, extending her hand. "I'm pleased to meet you after everything Euler told me."

"Just what has he told you?"

"About HAND, and what you've done to fight for the individual." There was a sad softness about her mouth as she spoke. "You've made it my fight too."

Euler Frost cleared his throat. "She's supplied us with a great deal of information about Nova. And best of all, she tipped me off when Earl Jazine came snooping around. We were able to follow her with Jazine and capture him in her bed."

Axman gazed down at the woman before him. "Oh?"

"Anything for the cause," she said with a shrug.

"Tell me about Stanley Ambrose."

"I knew him before he became head of the Venus Colony. I was his mistress."

"You must be very good in bed."

She blushed a bit. "He is a much older man, not hard to please."

"And he told you about Nova?"

"That's the odd part. He didn't tell me a thing. I haven't seen him since his return, or even heard from him in about two years."

Axman glanced at Frost. He didn't understand. "Then how were you able to convey this information about Nova?"

"I learned it from another source." She hesitated and then said, "From Jason Blunt."

"Blunt? The other man in this secret election?"

"Yes."

"What did Blunt tell you?"

"That Nova has an underground city in an old missile defense headquarters in Utah. That they have computerized the entire history of this country, with an aim toward preserving its past."

Graham Axman smiled slightly. "So you too believe that Nova presents a greater menace than our government."

"Yes. Their machines could make change impossible, and without change the nation would wither and die."

He nodded and seemed to wave her away with his hand. "Let us go in now to meet with the others."

The meeting of the HAND strike force, held within the bare, curving walls of an old grain warehouse on the deserted farm, did not go well for Graham Axman. He was well aware that the months of prison confinement had robbed him of his vigor, of his ability to concentrate on details and plan an operation. But now there was a new challenge to his authority in the person of Euler Frost. Most of the men who faced him and listened to his words had followed Frost in the months gone by. They had been with Frost when Jazine was kidnapped, and they had helped with the escape of Axman himself. They were ready to follow Euler Frost anywhere, but they knew Axman only as a former leader who'd gotten himself imprisoned.

Surprisingly, it was Venray who led the opposition to the White House plan, and Axman cursed the black man as he heard him ask, "Just what are the goals of HAND, and is this attack in keeping with those goals?"

"The goals of HAND, the goals of our Fellowship? I would have thought that Euler Frost might have instructed you in those during my enforced absence. HAND aims at nothing less than the reestablishment of the individual, the overthrow of the machine society which robs us of our individuality."

"But how is President McCurdy to blame for this?"

"He represents authority."

"And in his place, what would you put?"

Axman glanced around at the cornerless room, feeling himself imprisoned once more. The white plastoid walls seemed to shriek their control over him, and the faces of his followers could just as easily have been the faces of his jailers. "We want freedom for the individual," he stated, and then, echoing words he'd once heard Frost speak, he hurried on. "Let man take over from the machine. Let hands do honest work again."

"And let us face our real enemy," Frost interrupted. "That enemy is not in Washington but beneath the sands of the Utah desert. I propose that this strike force be aimed at Blunt and Ambrose and their underground city."

"How do we know such a city even exists?" Axman challenged. They were face to face now, like two debaters on a rostrum.

98

"You know the answer to that! Milly Norris told you she learned it from Blunt!"

"Milly Norris? She lured a Computer Cop into a trap. Why couldn't she be luring us into one too? Why couldn't she get us all into this underground city and then flood it, or blow it up? Then President McCurdy would have no more worries from HAND!"

It was a moment of decision, and for an instant Axman thought he had them. But then a few eyes turned toward Milly, who stood in the back against the curving plastoid wall of the granary. She did not say a word, but she didn't have to. Frost was doing the talking for her.

"Believe that if you will, but I will be leading the attack on Nova. If it is a trap, I'll be the first to die. Now you decide. Do you follow Axman to the New White House, or me to the desert of Utah?"

The meeting broke up soon after, without any firm decision. But Axman could feel his power slipping away. His leadership of HAND had been challenged, and things would never be the same again.

Unless he acted quickly.

Their rooms were in a dormitory adjoining the abandoned grain warehouse, and Milly Norris had been given a place there too. It was to her room that Axman made his way later that night, when he was certain Frost and the others slept.

"Who is it?" she asked through the door in response to his soft knocking.

"Graham Axman. I must talk to you."

"I . . ."

"Just for a moment."

She slid open the door and peered out, her face shadowed by the polarized light. "What do you want?"

"Let me in," he said, pushing past her. In that moment his motives were mixed even in his own mind. The possibility of sexual assault was certainly among them. "Now then, I want to know everything about this man Blunt."

"In the middle of the night?"

"Are we suddenly modest?"

She merely stared at him. "No, just sleepy."

"Then I won't keep you long. But it was never explained to me how you came in contact with Jason Blunt."

"He contacted me, if you must know." She seated herself on the edge of the cycled bed, crossing her legs so that the pale pink nightsuit fell open. His eyes took in the full thighs, slender calves, thin ankles.

"For what purpose?" he asked.

She glanced around nervously, and for an instant he was reminded of a laudanum addict seeking a dose. But then she seemed to settle down, facing him with a bland, bleak smile. "I was Stanley Ambrose's mistress, remember? It seems to be a fact that was well known around the country. I sometimes wonder that it wasn't on the telenews, or in the hologram theaters."

"Blunt came to you because of that?"

"Yes, he came to me because of that. The first time." She turned to gaze at the wall. "He wanted to know about Stanley, just as Euler Frost and Earl Jazine did later."

100

"You became Blunt's lover?"

She shrugged. "He bought a sixteen-year-old girl as a bride on the Turkish market. As you know, those things have a way of paling after a few years. He's a wealthy man, most generous with his gifts. I would have been foolish to refuse him. Stanley had stopped writing to me, after all."

"Had Ambrose ever mentioned Blunt in his letters?"

"No, and I really couldn't tell Jason anything he wanted to know. I learned a great deal from him, though."

"Which you passed along to Euler."

"Yes."

"How did he come into the picture?"

"The same as everyone else. He heard that Stanley might be involved in some plot, and found out that I was Stanley's mistress. The difference was that I liked Euler. He convinced me that HAND was on the right side, and so I began to supply him with information."

"Information you got from Blunt."

"Correct."

Axman shook his head. "And then you lured this Jazine into bed too? You really should have been a spy, a twenty-first-century Mata Hari!"

"There are some things that I do well," she admitted.

"Would you care to demonstrate?"

But she only laughed. "It's much too late for that. I am on Euler Frost's side in this, Mr. Axman."

"That could be the wrong side."

"We'll see."

She rose and saw him out. "Thank you for the information anyway," he said as the door closed behind him.

If he had gone there hoping to win an ally, he was disappointed. Euler Frost had beaten him again.

11.
JASON BLUNT

The flight to Utah with Carl Crader had been one of those necessary irritations with which one is often faced in the business world. To startle the enemy and show your hand to him was a risky business, but Blunt was used to taking risks. While still in his late twenties he'd bluffed a competitor out of an oil site in the Arctic Ocean by taking him for a submarine ride to inspect cold-weather drilling equipment. The man, convinced Blunt had unlimited resources, quickly backed away from the deal.

He'd tried something of the same technique with Carl Crader. No words he could speak would have impressed Crader nearly as much as the flight to the desert and a personally conducted tour of the underground city. The word would certainly get back to President McCurdy, and that was what Jason Blunt wanted.

In its early stages, Nova Industries had been entirely his idea. At that time there was no thought of building a new superstate out of the lessons of the past. The computer complex with its fabulous input and hundreds of highly skilled technologists was designed strictly as a business proposition. That was before the coming of Stanley Ambrose.

It was Ambrose who schemed and plotted, Ambrose who split the Nova employees into two factions, Ambrose who wanted an election. And once an election was agreed upon, it seemed only natural that it be conducted by computer.

Jason Blunt had no doubt as to the outcome of that secret election. Ambrose was in control from the beginning, and now he knew Ambrose would be traveling about the country notifying the others of the result. Blunt would be the last to know, and by then it would be too late to resist Stanley Ambrose's plans for conquest.

"Why did you show him all that?" Masha asked on the flight back to their island after depositing Crader at the Dallas International Jetport.

"Because it pleased me to do so."

"What about Ambrose and the others? Won't they be angry?"

"Let them be! I built that complex out there, and I don't intend to lose it to Ambrose because of some foolish election. He can do what he wants, but now Crader knows its location. If Ambrose tried to seize control of the government, McCurdy could destroy the whole thing with a few well-placed hydrobombs."

"It's dangerous, Jason."

"These days life is dangerous."

"Why not let Ambrose have it? There's still our island, and the drilling operations. You don't need computers for any of that."

"Masha, Masha . . ." He rumpled her hair as he would a child's. "You are so much a woman in some things, and yet still a youngster in others. Don't you

104

see, life today *is* computers! There's nowhere we could go on earth to escape the influence of the machines. Back on the island? In case you've forgotten, we have computerized drilling machinery, a computerized security system, even computerized climate control, thanks to the federal government. When you get out of bed in the morning and find your breakfast prepared, that's done by computer too!"

"But none of these depend upon those things back in Utah. That's my point, Jason—let Stanley Ambrose have the underground city!"

"I'll see it destroyed first."

Below, like a jewel of green in the blue of the Gulf, their island appeared. The rocketcopter dipped toward it, avoiding a flight of gulls that spiraled up from the water. In another moment they were on the ground.

Jason Blunt entered the big house and went immediately to the video where a printout of the afternoon news awaited him. Scanning the headlines and seeing nothing but the usual presidential campaign news, he transferred his attention to the message center. There were stock quotations and oil futures, along with a drilling report from a new island off South Africa that looked promising. But the thing that caught his eye was a one-sentence unsigned messagegram.

"Sunsite pioneers seek meeting at earliest convenience."

Sunsite.

It was from Milly Norris, and something had happened. She'd never contacted him by messagegram before, directly to his home. He ripped the plastic from the machine and stuffed it into his pocket.

Then he walked down the long hall to the solarium where Masha waited.

She was stretched on the floor, nude in the glow of afternoon sunlight, waiting to make love. It had become a ritual on days when he was home, harking back somehow to those early days of honeymooning aboard the *Strombol,* when everything was sunshine and sensuality.

"I must go away," he said quietly.

"Again, darling? But you've *been* away."

"It's business. There was a messagegram waiting for me."

"Business with Stanley Ambrose?"

"No. Oil business."

"Must you leave right now?"

He stared down at the curve of her thighs. "Yes."

"Oh, very well!" she sighed, rising slowly to her feet. She hugged him to her and gave him a long, deep kiss. "Hurry back!"

"I will," he promised.

He'd always hated Sunsite. There was something about the stolid framework of the town that reminded him once more of computer circuits. At least the old cities had a wonderfully unplanned look about them, a hodgepodge of streets and alleyways that he still found charming. There was nothing charming about Sunsite, not even the quaint old church in the town square.

Now, an hour after sundown, Milly Norris was waiting for him in the square by the church, watching a hologram band concert on one of the coin machines. She looked up as he approached and said,

"Imagine people going to the parks to hear real bands, Jason! Why don't they do it anymore?"

"Musicians are too expensive, like everything else."

"I suppose so."

"I got your message. Why so urgent?"

She snapped off the hologram and the image faded from around them. There was only the park once more, a bit drab despite the festive neon trim to the trees. "Something happened. I thought you should know about it."

"What?"

"A man named Earl Jazine came to see me. He's with the Computer Investigation Bureau."

"I know them," he said. "Jazine's boss called on me."

"They know about using the FRIDAY-404 for the secret election. They know that you and Stanley were the candidates."

"What else do they know?"

"That was about all, but Jazine sure asked a lot of questions."

"About Ambrose?"

"Certainly. I showed him the letters and holograms, and he made photocopies of them."

"Do the Computer Cops have any idea where Ambrose is?"

She shook her head. "No. But they're looking for him."

"So Jazine went away unhappy?"

"He was kidnapped."

Jason Blunt felt a tingle of fear. "Kidnapped? From where?"

"Well, from my bed, if you must know. He was just climbing in when these masked men with stunners burst into the apartment."

"God, you'll sleep with anybody!" He considered the possibilities of her story. It could be a lie, but there seemed no reason for her to make it up. "Who were the men?"

"I told you they were masked! They took Jazine away and that's the last I saw of him."

"How'd they know he was here?"

"Now how in hell should I know that? Do you think I told them?"

"I don't know," he answered honestly. "Sometimes I wonder just whose side you're really on, Milly."

"Is there another side besides yours?"

"Yes. There's always Stanley Ambrose."

She sighed in the darkness. "I told you I haven't seen him in six years."

"But I've seen him, Milly. He mentions you sometimes." He hesitated and then added, "Is it possible that five years on another planet could have deranged him somehow, lightened his brain cells?"

"I know a man who was on Venus ten years and he seems perfectly all right."

"Who's that?"

She looked away. "No one you know."

"Someone else you're sleeping with?"

Her eyes flashed, catching the neon reflection from the trees. "That's none of your damned business."

He thought, perversely, of Masha on the floor of the solarium, bathed in the afternoon sunlight. "Are we going up to your place?" he asked.

108

"The bed might be occupied."

"Stop it!"

"Go home and fuck one of your oil wells!"

He was silent for a moment. Then he said, "I'm sorry. I have no hold on you, no right to question your private life."

"Damn right!"

"Want to watch another band concert?"

"No." Softly. He wondered if she was crying, but in the dark he couldn't be sure.

"What, then?"

"Let's go back."

"To the apartment?"

"Yes."

They boarded a moving sidewalk and rode to her street. Standing beside her, Jason Blunt tried to puzzle out the meaning of it all. If someone had truly kidnapped Jazine, the CIB man, who had it been? Ambrose, perhaps? Or even that antimachine group, HAND? Maybe they were still around, as Carl Crader had implied.

Suddenly he reached a decision. "It could be dangerous back at your apartment. It was dangerous for Jazine last night."

"Where, then?"

"My rocketcopter is parked at the town airstrip. It has a bed."

"I don't do it in rocketcopters."

"You should try sometime."

"Goodnight, Jason. Take care."

"You're leaving me?"

"What you said is true. The apartment isn't safe."

"A motel, perhaps?"

"There are no motels in Sunsite. Everyone lives here, and nobody visits."

"You've had quite a few visitors lately."

"Not overnight."

They'd reached the sidewalk terminus, and she stepped off to enter her apartment. "I'll leave you here," he said. Already there was a gnawing fear deep in his stomach.

"Good-bye, then."

There was no kiss, no embrace. He stepped onto the opposite sidewalk and was borne away.

All the way back to the rocketcopter he half expected to encounter Stanley Ambrose, a shadowy figure who would inform him quite clearly that he had lost the election.

12.

MILLY NORRIS

On the Saturday of Graham Axman's daring escape, Milly Norris had read about it in the nightly telenewspaper. She'd called Frost on the visionphone at once.

"Euler, how are you?"

"Fine. Good to see you."

"Is this circuit safe?"

His familiar grin came back at her from the screen. "It is if anything is. I debugged it myself. If anyone tried a tap or a cut-through, the picture would scramble."

"I just read about Axman."

"Yeah. Really something, huh?"

"Were you there?"

"More or less. It was fun."

"Euler, I summoned Jason and told him about Jazine, just as you suggested. But I'm afraid he's stopped trusting me. He wouldn't come back to the apartment."

"Don't worry about it."

"Can I come there, where you are?"

"Sure. I want you to meet Axman, anyway. Better give us a few days, though. He needs some condition-

111

ing to recover himself. Prison hit him hard."

"I'll be there Wednesday."

"Fine," he said, and the screen went blank.

She leaned back in the chair and thought about Euler Frost. There had been many men in her life, even before Stanley. At the age of nineteen she'd fallen in with a band of Trekers, the remains of an old television fan club active in the late twentieth century. In their own way, the Trekers were much like the flippies of South New York, who painted their bodies and indulged in harmless orgies. A year with them, passed around among a circle of willing males, had been more than enough for Milly. After that she moved west to Sunsite, a quiet little town where everything was programmed—even, she sometimes thought, the sex.

She'd met Stanley Ambrose while he was teaching at the local university, after the death of his wife. The affair had been convenient for them both, and she'd never dreamed that it would lead to the present complications. First there'd been Jason Blunt, wealthy and willing, who'd come for information and stayed for a bit of loving. That had been shortly after Stanley returned to earth from his government service on Venus. Since she knew nothing about Stanley's present activities, she'd been a bit surprised when Jason kept up the relationship, even confiding bits and pieces of information about his business relationship with Stanley.

It had been that relationship which most interested Euler Frost when he appeared on the scene. And it was Euler who most interested her. He was younger than Jason, and handsomer in a rough-hewn way. If

112

he lacked the money to lavish expensive diamonds on her, he was still a man to be trusted. She told him about Stanley, and more—she told him about Blunt and his questions. She told him of Blunt's computerized dreams, and of the great underground city in the desert.

And when Earl Jazine appeared at her office that afternoon, her first thought was to warn Euler. He'd taken it from there, with the kidnapping and all that came after. He'd even suggested that she summon Jason to give him a full report. Euler was nothing if not devious.

Sitting back in her chair, still facing the blank screen of the vision-phone, she wondered what it would be like to meet Graham Axman. During these past months Euler's talk had been of little else, and now that Axman was free at last she had the feeling that momentous events were waiting to transpire.

Yes, Graham Axman.

He was a man to meet.

But then the meeting came, on that midweek evening, and she was vaguely disappointed. She was even more disappointed when Axman came to her room later that night to pump her for information. Was this the man Euler had wanted so badly to free from prison? This wild-eyed devil who planned to attack the New White House?

She expressed her misgivings to Euler the following morning at breakfast, while Graham Axman wandered alone out by the fields. "He wanted me, Euler. He wanted me against you. He wanted sex, and more than that."

"You may be exaggerating. He's been in prison for several months, and that might have contributed to his sexual frustrations, but he'll be all right."

"He hardly sounded like it yesterday. Euler, I believe in HAND, I believe in what you're fighting for, but Graham Axman will tear the organization apart! Before you know it you'll be bickering like Stanley Ambrose and Jason Blunt. You'll be holding your own secret election!"

"It's hardly gone that far," he said, trying to reassure her. "HAND is Graham's organization, after all. I'm sure he's only trying to do what he thinks is right."

"HAND *was* Graham's organization, Euler. Now it's yours. You have to lead it."

"We'll see."

Axman returned at that moment, striding through the sliding door of the little kitchen and rubbing his hands together. "It's brisk out there! Don't they have climate control in this part of the country?"

"Not this far out," Euler told him.

Axman took some coffee from the masterbrew. "How are you this morning, Milly? Have a good night's sleep?"

"Very good, thanks." She avoided his eyes, not knowing how much he might have overheard.

"A good night's sleep is what I needed. I'm beginning to shake off the prison pallor. A bit more sleep and sun and I'll be back to my old self."

Milly's eyes narrowed as she weighed his words. He did indeed seem improved from the previous evening, but she wondered if it was a true improvement or only some sort of act. Euler had told her once of

Axman's acting experience in his youth, when his father produced shows on the island of Plenish. His whole new attitude might be nothing more than the work of a clever actor.

But how was she to know?

"Glad to hear it," Euler was saying. "Do we go ahead, then?"

Axman nodded. "We'll start planning the attack on this underground computer complex. President McCurdy can wait."

They shook hands, and in Euler Frost's face Milly could see a reflection of old times.

But still she wondered.

She went back to Sunsite on the weekend, and settled into the office routine once more. It was not the busy period at the tax office—payment schedules were always planned so that nothing came due during the month before elections—and so she passed her time on Monday in conversation with the other programmers, thinking up elaborate lies to explain her absence of a few days.

That night, as she entered her apartment after a quick computerized dinner at the office, the vision-phone was buzzing. She answered it at once, expecting to see a girlfriend's familiar face. Instead, there was only a hazy blur on the screen. Some joker was covering the lens, which probably meant an obscene call.

"Milly—how are you?"

"Who is this?"

"Don't you recognize my voice, Milly?"

"No." And yet there was something about it . . .

"It's Stanley. Stanley Ambrose."

"My God! Let me see you!"

The haze fell away from the screen and her eyes focused on the dim, uncertain presence of Stanley Ambrose. How long had it been? Six years?

"How do I look, Milly?"

"I . . . don't know. Different."

"I want to see you."

"Sure. Where are you?"

"Here."

"In Sunsite?"

"Yes."

She could feel her heart thumping. Seeing old friends—old lovers—always affected her like this. "When can we get together?"

"Tonight. I want to see you tonight, Milly. Can you meet me?"

Panic gripped her as she sought for an excuse. "Gee, this is a rain night. We have climate control, and the rain is supposed to start around eleven."

"Milly, this is *Stanley*! I want to *see* you!"

"Well, hell, you've been back a year and now you're in a big rush all of a sudden! I'm supposed to drop everything and run off to meet you!"

"I can't explain it, Milly. I've had some business matters."

"I heard about them."

"You did? From where?"

"We'll talk about it. Where are you?"

"In the amusement area. I'm calling from a booth near the rocket ride."

"Can't you come here?"

"I think your place is being watched, Milly. I have

116

many enemies these days."

"All right. I'll be there in thirty minutes."

She remembered to wear her waterproof cape in the event she wasn't back before the eleven o'clock rain started. These things weren't exact, and on some Monday nights the rain had been known to begin nearly an hour early.

The streets of Sunsite were almost empty as she took the moving sidewalk to the amusement area. Monday was never a big night for going out, and since it had been designated a rain night there was one more reason to keep people at home. As she neared the amusement area on the south side of the town the sidewalk became a bit more crowded, mostly with teen-age girls in bodysuits and dyed hair, prowling in groups while waiting for the boys to appear. Among teen-agers there was always action, even on rain nights. It made her think of her own teen years, and then surprisingly of Earl Jazine. She'd known him so briefly, but he was something like the boys she used to date, before the Treker days.

There were few older people at the amusement area, and she wondered why Stanley had picked it for a meeting place. Moving past the pneumatic merry-go-round and the gravity house, she tried to get her bearings. Without children, and too old to date the teen-age boys, she'd had little reason to come here. The place was strange to her, a dream of strobe lights and screaming kids and signs that urged one to *Walk on the Moon Just Like Spacemen* or *Experience Anti-Gravity for Only a Dollar!* It was like another planet, but perhaps that was its purpose.

117

She passed the mirror maze and the electric tumble, and finally spotted the rocket ride she sought. At first she saw no one resembling Stanley Ambrose, but then as she neared her destination he stepped out from the shelter of a dime-up machine.

"Hello, Milly."

"Stanley." Her eyes tried to focus on him in the garish light, but she could see only a pleasant, smiling figure who seemed to have no relation to her. He'd lost weight, and his face was drawn, and when he spoke his voice had an odd, far-off quality.

"It's good to see you again."

"Stanley, where have you been so long?"

"I'm engaged in some secret activities. I've had to live underground."

"Underground? In an underground city?"

"You know about that?"

There was something wrong, something with his voice. It was almost as if she were speaking to a robot. "Yes, I know about it," she said, and reached out to touch his hand, to reassure herself that he was indeed human.

"What else do you know?"

"The election—I heard about that. Did you win?"

He didn't answer.

"Stanley—why did you want to see me again?" She wished now that she had phoned Euler before leaving the apartment. Euler—or even Jason Blunt. Somebody!

"I had to find out whose side you were on, Milly. There are sides to everything these days, you know."

"I was on your side for a long time, Stanley. But you deserted me, remember?"

118

"You could have come with me to Venus."

The rocket ride had started up again, igniting his ashen face with the reflection of bright orange fire. "No. No, I couldn't have done that," she mumbled.

"What is it? What's the matter?"

"Nothing. It's just that you're a stranger to me, Stanley. It's as if I didn't know you. I guess six years is too long a time."

Too long.

"I'm the same person, Milly."

No, you're not!

"No, you're not, Stanley. None of us stay the same. We grow and mature and drift apart."

"There's someone else, isn't there?"

"Not really. I didn't stay celibate waiting your return, if that's what you mean. But there's no one person. No one who'll ever be as close to me as you were."¹

His right hand dipped into his pocket and came out holding an electric lighter. He fumbled for a short cigar and lit it quickly. She watched the hand as it deposited the lighter in an inner pocket and returned to view. "Smoking," he mumbled by way of explanation. "These damned cigars are one more bad habit I acquired on Venus."

"Yes." She had to get away. Somehow she had to escape from him.

"You seem terribly nervous. Is that what seeing me again does to you?"

A voice cut through the night, suddenly all around them. *"Attention please! The amusement area will close in ten minutes due to rain night! We repeat, the amusement area will close in ten minutes!"*

"I have to go," she said quickly. "The rain will be starting."

"Wait." He put out his hand to touch her, but she backed away.

"It was good seeing you again, Stanley. Good seeing you. Too bad we couldn't . . ."

She turned and started to run, losing herself in the departing crowd. When she paused to look back he was gone, and she sighed with relief.

Now to get out of here and back to the apartment. She'd be safe there, and she could phone Euler. The crowd was thinning, almost all gone. She'd have to hurry.

The first drop of rain hit her forehead.

Damn! Early again! A full half hour early! She hurried toward the exit and the moving sidewalk that would take her home.

That was when she saw the man with the tattooed face. He was standing by the exit gate with both hands plunged deep into his pockets. He seemed to be waiting for someone, and in that instant—seeing her—he began to move forward.

She glanced around, looking for help, but there was none. The place was deserted, with the last of the stragglers scattered by the rain. Even Stanley was gone. It was as if the earth had swallowed them all up.

Tears of rain blurred her vision. Don't panic, she told herself. Just don't panic. Perhaps this is a different tattooed man, not the one who tried to kill Earl Jazine. Surely more than one person in the country had a tattoo on his face. Surely . . .

The closest building was the mirror maze, and she

120

ran to that. The thick slabs of glass were unbreakable here, tempered to withstand a stunner's blast or even an old-fashioned bullet. It was the safest place she could be, really, behind this unbreakable glass where he could see her but never reach her.

She darted through the entrance and slid the glass door shut behind her, locking it. He was still coming toward her, but he wouldn't be for long. The glass would protect her.

But still he came, walking slowly, and she retreated farther into the maze, putting extra layers of glass between them but still keeping him in view.

She looked around, seeking some alarm switch, or at least a light switch which could cloak her in darkness, but they were back by the door. Too far away.

He was at the glass now, and even at this distance she could see the bright curving tattoo around his left cheek. Perhaps it covered a scar, or marked him as an eastern prince. Perhaps if she knew him she wouldn't be terrified at all.

All over the amusement area, the neons and strobes were beginning to die, blinking out as some unseen hand worked a switch. In another moment the mirror maze would be dark too, and then he could no longer look in through the glass at her.

Another minute.

No longer.

She saw his hand come out of the pocket, as Stanley's had done. Only this hand held a weapon, a squat little gun—too small to be a stunner.

She recognized it just as the tattooed man pulled the trigger, and by then it was too late to run.

The laser beam passed through the layers of glass

without breaking them, seeking her out with unerring accuracy. She tried to scream as it hit her, but there was no time now.

No ti——

13.
CARL CRADER

Even when the news of Graham Axman's daring escape reached him, Crader did not alter his routine. It was a Saturday, after all, and he'd promised to spend the weekend at home with his wife.

"Don't worry," he told Jazine on the vision-phone. "You warned the prison. We did everything we could."

"But he's out, chief. He's back with HAND."

"Keep me advised of developments. For now we just sit tight."

"Right, chief," Jazine said with a sigh and switched off.

Crader left the vision-phone and went back outside to the patio, where his wife was enjoying one of the last warm weekends of fall. "More work, dear?" she asked from her vibrochair.

"Not really. Nothing that need concern me today."

"That's good. Let some of the younger men handle things for a change."

He grunted and returned to his video viewer. He'd been running a cassette of the 2036 Olympic Games, but now it was difficult to concentrate on the run-

123

ning, jumping figures. He thought about HAND, and about Graham Axman once more in control.

It was an opinion he had never communicated even to Jazine, much less to the President, but Carl Crader believed there was a great deal of good in the goals of Humans Against Neuter Domination. He had believed it ever since his first encounter with Euler Frost on the island of Plenish during the transvection affair, and it was an opinion that had been strengthened during the HAND raid on the Federal Medical Center. He allowed Frost to escape that time, in the smoke and confusion of the moment, and he'd never regretted that decision. The machines really were taking over the country—not in the sudden dramatic revolt of science fiction dreams, but rather in a slow, insidious seepage that every year, every *day*, robbed the human being of one more shred of self-esteem.

Axman was, to some extent, an unknown quantity. But Crader was willing to put his trust in Euler Frost. Even a few bombed machines now might be preferable to a society that would awaken one morning to find its free will programmed into the memory unit of a computer.

So he worried very little about the escape that weekend. Even on Monday, when one of the presidential advisers reached him by vision-phone, inquiring about it, Crader only referred him to another department. Certainly the escape itself was not a matter for the CIB. What might come after the escape, once Axman and Euler Frost joined forces again, was another matter.

During the week that followed, his mind was taken

up with other matters. A complex scheme to swindle a midwestern bank through the use of forged voice-print commands to the bank's computer had been uncovered, and it took a full two days of staff work to sort out just what happened. Then too, there was the matter of the FRIDAY-404 system, with President McCurdy still expressing concern about the election only a few weeks away.

By week's end, Earl Jazine brought in a favorable report on the election system. "Professor Friday has gone over every component, chief. It's working perfectly. You can tell the President he doesn't have a thing to worry about."

Crader was pleased to hear it. "Fine!"

"A funny thing, though, chief."

"About the computer?"

"No, something else." He sank into the foamfold chair opposite Crader's desk. "I thought I should check on that girl I was with when HAND pulled off the kidnap hoax."

"Milly Norris?"

"Yeah. If she was in on it, I figured she might tell me something about HAND. If she wasn't, I wanted to see if she was all right."

"And complete your business with her?" Crader asked with a grin.

"No. Hell, it was just a loose end."

"I know."

"Anyway, she's not there."

"Not where?"

"In Sunsite. She's been away from work since Tuesday, and she's not at her apartment either."

"A vacation, perhaps."

"Without telling them at work? She just called Wednesday morning and told her boss she had to go away for a few days."

"You think it's tied in with Axman's escape?"

"I think so, chief."

Crader thought about it. "If she's with HAND, then she's the one who's been supplying Frost his information. But where is the information coming from? Has she been seeing Stanley Ambrose after all?"

"Nobody else has, that's for sure!"

"Well, keep checking on her. If she comes back, try to find out where she's been."

Earl Jazine nodded. "Meanwhile, what are we doing about Jason Blunt's underground city?"

"Not enough," Crader admitted ruefully. "I'm glad you asked me before the President did. I think I'll try to reach Blunt on the vision-phone."

But Masha only told him that Jason Blunt was away on another of his frequent journeys. He might be back on Sunday, or Monday. And so it was the first of the week before Crader finally reached him, and Tuesday before he flew out for another meeting at the underground city.

By that time, Jazine had brought word of Milly Norris's murder by laser gun, in the amusement area at Sunsite.

For a time Crader considered postponing his flight to Utah and going to Sunsite instead, but finally he agreed that Jazine could handle things with the local police.

"Check on any strangers who might have arrived

in town," he told Earl. "And especially check for anyone answering Graham Axman's description."

"You really think Axman killed her?"

"No, but someone's sure to raise the possibility. I just don't want to miss anything."

Jazine thought about it. "She was pretty easy to get into bed. It might have been a crime of passion—jealousy, something like that."

"With a laser gun? Maybe, but I doubt it."

"When will you be back from Utah?"

"Who knows?" Crader said with a dry chuckle. "They might kidnap me and seal me up in a computer."

"If that happens I'll call out the army and come rescue you."

"Good! I'll be relying on that."

They shook hands as if departing for distant planets and Crader went up the stairs to the rocketcopter pad.

The flight west was pleasantly relaxing, and he spent the time reviewing staff reports on the Utah facility and its history. The government in Washington had all but forgotten the existence of the underground city, supposing after its sale to Nova Industries that the space was being used for the storage of natural gas. Even the shipment of computer components and vast supplies to the site from Nova's eastern plants had apparently passed unnoticed.

As for Nova Industries itself, the government reports had little to offer. Originally a wholly owned subsidiary of Blunt's underwater oil-drilling company, Nova had been reorganized a year ago as a separate corporation whose major stockholders were

Jason Blunt and Stanley Ambrose. There the record stopped.

Crader grunted and put away the files. Below him, on the transcontinental expressway, he could see the tiny dots of electric cars moving like ants through the tan and sandy stretches of desert. He was almost there, almost back to the dry lake bed that concealed the entrance to Nova's underground city.

Jason Blunt was already there, and he greeted Crader at the elevator. "I hardly expected to see you back here so soon," he said, shaking hands. "Do you have a message from our President?"

"In a way," Crader replied, improvising. "He's very much interested in your computer center here, but somehow he's not reassured about your motives. He'd like me to inspect the place a little more carefully."

"Inspect? You mean search it? Do you think we have little men hidden inside the machines?"

"Hardly, but you may have something else hidden there. It's one thing to computerize past events in a memory unit. It's quite another to program your machines with a learning power by which they could control future events. A close examination of the wiring can show me just what you've done."

"I'm certain you'll find nothing, but come down to my office and we'll talk about it," Blunt said.

They descended by elevator to a room Crader had only glimpsed on his first visit. It was a luxuriously appointed office, with high, radiant ceiling, foamfold chairs, a white shag rug, and a console desk that looked like the keyboard of a giant organ. On one
128

wall hung a chart of the underground city, color-coded for seven different zones of activity.

"Quite a place," Crader marveled. "I wish the government could afford something like this for me!"

"I can control input from here, and also get readouts on any of the programmed information. Though of course in actual practice our computer specialists do all the work."

Crader slipped into an especially comfortable chair and watched Blunt pass a comb through the fringes of his black beard. "But you do exercise some control over input."

Blunt shrugged. "Stanley Ambrose has a great deal to do with it too. I can't swear that his people haven't set up an entire program that's unknown to me."

"Has Ambrose been here recently?"

"He's in and out."

"Strange that you've seen him and no one else has."

"That's his way when he's working on a project."

"Just what is the project?"

"You know—this election business."

Crader nodded. "How many employees did you say Nova had?"

"I didn't, but there are two hundred here. Counting employees, stockholders and their families, there are over eighty thousand. My oil drilling people are included too. All of them voted in our election."

"And of those stationed here, how many would you say are loyal to you and how many to Ambrose?"

"The split is about even."

"The figures we found in the FRIDAY-404 computer showed some forty-five thousand votes for Ambrose and thirty-six thousand for you."

Jason Blunt shrugged and did not seem surprised. "I had already assumed I lost the election."

"If Ambrose is around so little, how did he attract such a following?"

"The computer programmers got to know him, of course. And the others know him by reputation. He had a good deal of publicity during his years on Venus."

"But the programmers who supported him—certainly they would have done anything he ordered, even without your knowledge."

"I suppose so," he admitted.

"Then it's more important than ever that I be allowed to run my check on the wiring and circuits."

"Do you have any idea of the enormity of the task? We have miles of tunnels and conduits, holding enough wiring to reach the moon and back. It would take your entire bureau a month to inspect it all."

"I know where to look for what I want," Crader assured him.

"Very well," Blunt said after a moment's hesitation. "I'll show you whatever you want. Believe me, if you find the sort of evidence you're talking about, I'll confront Stanley with it. It's time we had a few things out anyway."

"It may be too late to confront him, if he's grown as powerful as I suspect."

"He's not that powerful."

Crader thought of something. "In such a highly computerized operation as this, surely your own employees are rated and assigned by computer too."

"Of course."

"If Ambrose was in control, what would prevent him from rigging the computer to have employees loyal to him transferred here, and employees loyal to you moved elsewhere?"

Jason Blunt frowned at the words. "There have been a number of transfers lately. I thought nothing of it, but . . ."

"Ambrose had a mistress, a woman named Mildred Norris."

"Oh?"

"Did he ever mention her to you?"

"He might have."

"She was murdered last night."

Blunt's hand jerked away from his beard. "My God!"

"You're startled. Did you know her?"

"No!"

"Then why does the news of her murder affect you like that? You're trembling, man!"

Blunt brought himself under control. "Violent death always affects me. Who killed her?"

"We don't know. It happened at an amusement park near her home. Somebody shot her with a laser gun."

"Why are you telling me this?"

"Because she's the second person to die during this investigation. A technician named Rogers was murdered too. Any of us could be next—you or me or anybody. If you know anything . . ."

Jason Blunt turned his back. "I knew the woman. I knew Milly. I met her a few times."

"When did you see her last?"

"A week or so ago. Maybe ten days."

"When did Ambrose see her last?"

"Not for years. She was in his past."

Something clicked for Crader. "Then you were her source of information. You told her about Nova and she passed the information on to HAND."

"HAND?"

Crader nodded. "Milly Norris had a great many friends, it seems."

"If I'd known she was passing information to HAND . . ."

"You'd have killed her?"

"No!"

"I was just completing the sentence for you. Somebody killed her, and the most likely suspects now seem to be you or Ambrose or one of the HAND people."

"That one who escaped from prison last week— Axman."

"Perhaps. We're looking into that possibility. Meanwhile, the best thing you can do is take me around your underground city. Not the tourist show like last time, but behind the scenes."

The bearded man sighed. "Very well. Follow me."

But the task of inspecting the wiring was not as simple as Crader had imagined. Behind the first bank of computers they entered a dim, narrow tunnel that led to a mass of exposed wiring. The various systems were easily recognizable, but the sheer bulk of it was enough to stagger him.

"It might take another man after all," he admitted.

132

"Or ten or twelve."

"But this isn't what I wanted anyway. These are memory cores. I want the reasoning capabilities—the game-playing, if you will."

Blunt led the way down another long corridor, past white-suited men and women working silently at their tasks. Except for the occasional hum of an electronic keyboard, there was very little noise deep down here in the earth.

"These are the units you want," Blunt said at last, stopping before a metal door with weld-bolts in place. "But the door has a twenty-year seal on it."

"What's that?"

"Certain units must be dustproofed and protected from human radiation. When they're units which will never need servicing, we place a twenty-year seal on the door to safeguard them."

"Break the seal," Crader said. "I want to look in there."

"All you'll find is a maze of wiring tunnels and socketboards running for miles. You could get lost in there."

"I won't get lost. Open up."

"I can't go with you. One's bad enough. Two of us could generate a dangerously high level of body heat."

Crader nodded. "I have a wrist-light. Break the seal and I'll go alone."

Jason Blunt hesitated another moment. Then he did as Crader asked and the door slid open on well-oiled tracks. Crader peered into the soft transitube glow ahead and snapped on his wrist-light. He had gone about ten feet into the tunnel when he heard the door slide closed behind him. The implication didn't bother him. He hardly believed that Blunt was prepared to seal him in here forever, and he could certainly create enough damage with these circuits to get himself freed in time if that move became necessary.

He went on down the tunnel, pausing here and there to remove and inspect a memory bank or relay system. The thing was complex in the extreme, but before long he found what he wanted. He recognized the configuration of circuits he'd studied many times before. Here was definite evidence of an attempt to duplicate the behavior and reasoning abilities of man. This was no mere storehouse of the past, but an artefact constructed to learn, to show homeostasis, and ultimately to rule.

Crader backed away, letting his wrist-light sweep farther along the passageway. Then, as he was about to start back toward the closed door, the light picked out a flicker of white. It was something low, near the floor . . .

He walked on a few paces, hardly believing the trick his eyes were playing on him. Something white . . .

And then he saw it clearly.

Here, on the floor of this sealed passageway at the back of a huge computer complex, rested the bones of a human skeleton.

14.

MASHA BLUNT

As soon as her nostrils detected the familiar harsh odor of those soilweed cigars, she knew that Stevro was back. And that was odd, because she hadn't even thought of him in the better part of a year.

She walked through the sliding lucite doors to the south patio and there he was, as brash and shabby as he'd always been. For just an instant, seeing him here in the unfamiliar setting of Sargasso unnerved her. But she recovered to say, "Hello, Stevro. It's been a long time."

He moved his bulk with the jerky motions she remembered so well. "You are more beautiful than ever, Masha."

"Thank you. And you are more ugly than ever."

He chuckled softly. "Three years have made you a shrew already. But I see they have made you a wealthy shrew." He glanced around in open admiration at the big house of glass and steel.

"What brings you halfway around the world, Stevro? Did the supply of young girls run out in New Istanbul?"

"Hardly," he answered with a dry chuckle. "There were some irregularities with the Turkish police, and

135

I thought it wise to move on. Naturally, since I was passing through the area, I had to stop for a visit with my Masha."

"I'm not your Masha anymore, Stevro. You sold me to Jason, remember?"

"Dear girl . . ."

"Never mind. Come in and I'll give you a drink. Standing out here on the patio you look as if you're casing the place for a robbery."

He followed her inside, marveling at the decor. "This place is worth a very large fortune, Masha dear. Is your husband about?"

"He's gone west on business, but there are servants," she said by way of warning. "And the drilling technicians at the end of the island, of course."

"The gear is so quiet!"

"The actual drilling goes on seven hundred feet beneath us. We rarely hear a thing." She walked to the wall bar and pressed a series of buttons for some premixed drinks. "How was your ride on the sea-rail? I assume that's how you arrived."

"Of course! I could hardly afford to hire a rocket-copter or a boat." He took out another of his soil-weed cigars. She could see that he was already mildly high from their effects. "The ride was pleasant. I sat with a man on his way to Panama for the fiesta."

She handed him his drink. "Just what do you want, Stevro? Is it money?"

"Masha . . ."

"Let's cut out the games. I like to see old friends, but you're not one of them. I was strictly a business proposition to you."

He smiled slightly, as if in memory. "And the
136

most successful business proposition of my life."

"Then it is money you want."

"But not from you. I have some information your husband might find valuable."

"I doubt that."

"Information about his oil-drilling operations in the Mediterranean. Think that might interest him?"

Masha studied him in the afternoon sunlight that poured through the great glass windows. As long as his visit concerned her she felt free to order him from the house at any time, but now he had cleverly shifted the emphasis to Jason—and to Jason's business operations.

"You'll have to call at some time when he's home," she said quietly. "It was foolish of you to make the trip here without calling first."

"Ah, but I wanted to see you in any event."

"You've seen me. Now you can go."

He shifted in his chair, holding the drink in one hand and his soilweed cigar in the other. "Could you contact your husband? It's important that I talk with him."

She wanted to say no, but the vision-phone was at her elbow and she knew full well that Jason was in Utah, available within seconds. "All right," she agreed finally. "I'll try to call him."

Within a minute the face of a pert, pretty secretary was on the screen. "Yes, Ms. Blunt. Your husband is here. Right now he's inspecting the facilities with Mr. Crader."

"Could you call him to the phone, please? It's important."

"Just a moment."

Masha saw the secretary turn in her chair and activate a remote paging system. There was a wait of perhaps three minutes before Jason's face appeared on the screen.

"What is it, Masha?" He sounded exasperated. "I'm very busy."

"Jason, remember Stevro, from New Istanbul? He's here on Sargasso, to see you."

"I don't have time to talk to him now!"

"He says it's important—about your Mediterranean drilling island."

She saw his features tighten with interest. "All right, put him on."

Stevro grinned slightly and took his place before the screen. "How are you, Mr. Blunt? Good to talk with you again."

"What is it, Stevro? I'm very busy here."

"You have a drilling island in the Mediterranean, I believe? Near Crete?"

"Yes."

"I can give you some information about that island, and about why your oil output there has fallen off in recent months."

"Well? Why has it?"

Stevro smiled and shook his head. "No, no, Mr. Blunt. I am a businessman like yourself. I sell my information."

"Damn it, man, I haven't got time to fool with you!"

"Let me come there, where you are, and we will make a little business deal."

On the screen Jason shook his head. "Either give

138

me the information or forget it. I haven't time for games."

"I can tell you one thing. My information concerns a man named Stanley Ambrose."

Jason Blunt was silent, thinking. Then he said, "Masha?"

"Yes, dear."

"Masha, call for the rocketcopter. I want you to fly out here with Stevro."

"Today?"

"Right now. You can be here in a few hours. I'll be waiting for you."

"All right." She flipped off the set and turned to Stevro. "You heard him. I guess he thinks it's important."

"Where are we going?"

"You wouldn't believe it if I told you."

Jason Blunt was indeed waiting for them. He ushered Masha and Stevro into his private office and seated himself at the great console facing them.

"Now then, what is all this business?"

"Quite a place you got here," said Stevro, looking around. "Is it all underground?"

"Never mind the place. I brought you out here for business. How much to tell me what you know?"

"A quarter-million."

"Ridiculous!"

Stevro shrugged and said nothing. Masha took the opportunity to ask, "Where's Carl Crader?"

Blunt turned his eyes toward her in surprise, as if he'd forgotten her presence in the room. "Crader is locked away. He wanted to inspect the circuits, so

I'm letting him. With luck he may be lost in there for days."

"In where?"

"The wiring tunnels behind the main computer bank. They run on for miles."

As her husband turned his attention back to Stevro, Masha left the office and made her way along the narrow sloping corridor. Soon she was in the main computer room, trying to remember the layout of the place from her single previous visit.

"Can I help you, Ms. Blunt?" one of the white-suited technicians asked.

"The wiring tunnels. Where is the main one?"

"Down the corridor to your left, but that's all sealed."

She nodded and went the way he'd directed. It seemed suddenly very important that she find Carl Crader, though she couldn't consciously explain the reason for her concern.

The corridor at this point seemed hewn out of solid rock, with a primeval look that contrasted sharply with the trim, modern lines of the computers. She hesitated, seeking a clue on the luminous wall signs, and then continued. The door, when she finally found it, was latched but not sealed. She slid it open and entered the dimness of the tunnel.

It was an eerie world of half-light, throbbing in the glow from the computer panelboards. Guided by that, and seeing very little else in the near darkness, she made her way along the tunnel.

"Carl Crader," she called once, and stopped, waiting for a reply. When none came, she moved a bit farther along the tunnel.

140

"Carl Crader!" Louder this time, so that her voice carried and echoed through the labyrinths ahead.

"Here! This way!" came an answering shout.

She found him finally deep down one of the side passages, guided by the glow from his wrist-light. "I never expected to find you in this maze," he said.

"I came to rescue you, but now I think we're both lost."

He smiled at that. "I can get out any time I want to, just by pulling a few of these circuits. They'd come for me fast enough!"

"Then you know the way back?"

"I think so. Come on. I've seen enough here anyway."

Outside, back in the corridor with the white-suited technicians, Masha led the way to Jason's office. He was still talking with Stevro, but he broke off in midsentence as they entered.

"Well, good to see you again, Crader. Find what you wanted in there?"

"I found quite a bit in three hours."

"Good! This is Mr. Stevro, an old friend of Masha's."

Stevro rose to shake hands, moving his bulk in the manner of a tired fighter. She wondered how the discussions had been going, but could tell nothing from her husband's face.

"I've heard about you," Stevro told Crader. "Computer Cops."

"We have other names too."

Stevro turned back to Jason. Apparently he wasn't about to be put off by their arrival on the scene. "Well, then, Blunt—how about it?"

141

Jason ran his fingers over his pointed black beard. "The sum is agreeable on one condition. That you remain here till tomorrow and confront Stanley Ambrose with your information."

Carl Crader appeared startled. "Ambrose is coming here?"

Jason nodded. "I just heard from him. He'll be here in the morning, and then maybe we'll get this thing straightened out."

"What thing?"

"The secret election. And other matters." He shot a look at Stevro.

"I have my own questions for Stanley Ambrose," Crader said. "I'd like to stay and meet him in the morning."

"What questions would those be?"

Crader's face was grim. "I can ask you the same ones, Blunt. My tour of the tunnel was very interesting. In addition to some circuited learning capabilities, I found a much more ancient evil."

"Learning capabilities?" Blunt repeated, looking blank. "I know of nothing like that." And then, as if the words were just catching up to him, he asked, "What ancient evil?"

"Murder. There's a human skeleton in that tunnel. The skull has been crushed by a blow. I'd like to know who it is, and how he died."

"A skeleton? In the computer?"

"In the wiring tunnel. Yes, I suppose you could say it's in the computer."

Masha was staring from one to the other, trying to grasp what was happening. "All right," she heard her

142

husband say. "You'll stay here too. And in the morning we'll all have questions for Stanley Ambrose."

15.

EARL JAZINE

Earl was late leaving the office that night, and he was still there when Carl Crader's call came through on the vision-phone from Utah. His face was a bit blurred on the screen, and as Jazine tried to adjust the focus, Crader said, "I didn't think I'd find you there this late. I was going to tape a message for you."

"A long day, chief. I was trying to find out something on the Norris killing, but the police didn't have a thing."

"Keep at it."

"How's it going out there?"

"Confusing, at the moment. Ambrose is due here in the morning, so I'm spending the night. There's something I want you to look into, though."

"Fire away." Jazine pressed the button of the electric pad to bring a fresh sheet of paper into position on his desktop.

"Nova Industries," Crader said, speaking softly. "You were successful breaking into their Chicago office. How about trying their plant in Kentucky?"

Jazine nodded. "Looking for what, chief?"

144

"We have a dead man here—or a skeleton."

"A what?"

"You heard me—a skeleton. Inside the computer, in one of the service tunnels. The door had a twenty-year seal on it, so I suppose whoever put him there felt safe. Anyway, the only bit of evidence other than bones is a torn piece of label from Nova's plant in Lexington, Kentucky. I've shown it to Jason Blunt, and we suspect the man may have been killed in Lexington and shipped west in an aircarton of computer parts."

"Why not just bury him?"

"That's one of the mysteries. That, and who it is. I want you to get inside the Lexington plant, if you can, and have a look at their personnel file. I need names of any employees who left or disappeared during the past year, when this tunnel was completed and sealed."

"Chief?"

"Yes?"

"If Blunt is with you on this, why can't he get the information? It's his company, isn't it?"

"Not the Lexington facility. That's Ambrose territory. And Blunt says he guards it well."

Jazine nodded. "I'm on my way."

On the way out of the office he saw the radiant ceiling still glowing in Judy's cubicle. "You still here too?" she asked.

"Call from the chief, out in Utah."

"How's he doing?"

"Good. Spending the night out there. Meanwhile, he's got a job for me. I need someone to copter down to Kentucky with me."

"Tonight?"

"If possible. Think we could rouse Mike Sabin?"

She glanced up at him, rabbiting her nose. "How about me? I could go."

"You?"

"Why not? Remember the time we crashed that flippie rally together?"

He considered it for a moment, weighing the dangers against the advantage of a fast start. They could leave now, do it tonight, without having to track down Sabin and get him to the office. "It could be dangerous," he warned. "I'm breaking into the Nova plant."

"Just working for the CIB is dangerous, with some of you guys around the office."

"All right," he agreed. "Let me pick up my gear. Call for the rocketcopter."

"How soon?"

He glanced at his digital watch. "Fifteen minutes. That should get us there by ten."

"Do you know anything about the layout of the Nova plant?"

"No, but that's easy. If they hold a government contract—and who doesn't these days?—their floor plan must be on file in Washington. Call it up on the telecopier and get us a clear print. Nova Industries, Lexington, Kentucky."

"Right, chief!"

"Don't call me that."

"Sorry. You sounded just like him."

Jazine grinned and went off to the supply room for the gear he would need. Twenty minutes later they were airborne over Manhattan, heading south

146

through the night sky.

Jazine worked quickly on the proximity gate of the Nova plant, shorting out the wires so they could walk through undetected. Both of them were dressed in black bodysuits, and they kept to the shadows of the landscaped lawn. With the increased use of proximity devices for plant security, the old floodlit grounds had become a thing of the past, so there was little worry about being seen as they crossed the grounds. The guards inside would rely on electronic devices, and that was their weakness.

"Are you going in?" Judy whispered at his side.

Jazine nodded. "You stay here and watch the energy alarm. Call me on the beeper if the needle starts moving."

The energy alarm was a particularly useful device in situations like this. Operating on an induction principle, it could pick up any sudden surge of power in the area. Thus a silent alarm or an electronic peeping device, or even sudden vision-phone activity, would cause the needle to jump. At this time of night such a power surge would mean his movements had been detected—or at least that security guards were suspicious. Since the energy alarm operated best outside of buildings, free from interference, Jazine needed someone to watch it while he went about his business inside.

"Be careful," she said as he moved off.

"Don't worry."

The emergency door at the rear of the building yielded quickly to his pocket magno, and he found himself inside the Nova plant. The printout of the

147

floor plan had already told him that the personnel office was down the corridor on the left. He entered it with ease, using the magno, and directed his wristlight at the personnel computer.

After five minutes of work he'd plugged the computer into a portable power source he carried on his belt, and switched it on. He could not use the wall plug, because the power surge would affect the needle on Judy's energy alarm and block out any energy from guard devices or vision-phones. He held his breath until the computer started delivering printouts, then directed it to give him the names of all employees who'd left the company during the past year.

The list was a short one, and he tore it off the roll to stuff into his pocket. Then, as he disconnected the computer from his portable power source and reconnected it to the wall outlet, the beeper vibrated against his body. Judy was warning him. Something was wrong.

Jazine sucked in his breath and sprinted for the emergency door. He found Judy on the other side, holding the energy alarm with its wildly fluctuating needle.

"They know we're here!" she gasped.

"Damn!" He took the box from her, trying to steady the needle, but already they could hear the footfalls of running security guards along the paved driveway.

Jazine pulled her back into the shadows as an armed guard trotted by. "There's someone on the grounds," he shouted to a companion. "They set off a pressure alarm."

148

Jazine cursed under his breath. A pressure alarm was like a landmine, and Judy had stepped on one while she waited for him.

"Do we take them alive?" one guard asked.

"Negative. Use your laser. Orders are to kill intruders on sight."

Judy gripped him in panic. "My God, Earl— what'll we do?"

"Try for the front gate, and hope it's not guarded."

But he knew it would be, and it was. A dozen laser-equipped guards were already fanning out from it, searching the grounds.

"Can we climb a tree?"

He glanced up. "The limbs are all too far from the ground."

"Then what's left? Just run for it?"

"They'd cut us down with their laser guns." His eyes were on the circle of lights gradually closing in on them.

"Earl—they wouldn't shoot a CIB agent, would they?"

"I'd never have a chance to show my badge, and even if I did they might kill us anyway. We're trespassers, remember."

"Over this way," someone shouted, and the lights began turning in their direction. They had set off another pressure alarm.

"Earl, I'm scared."

"You and me both." He glanced behind him but there were lights in that direction too. Suddenly he told Judy, "Take off your clothes! Quickly!"

"*What?*"

"Off with the bodysuit, and panties too if you're wearing any."

"Are you crazy?"

But he was already shedding his own suit. She stared at him for an instant and saw that he was serious. Her fingers moved to the zip, and the black vinyl fell away from her creamy body.

"All right, down on your back and spread your legs. At least we'll die happy!"

She started to speak but he came down on top of her, muffling her words. In another instant the beam from a wrist-light targeted them.

"What's this?" a guard shouted. "They're not spying—they're only fucking!"

Jazine broke away from Judy, trying to cover himself. The security guards gathered around for a look. They still held their laser guns, but most of the weapons were pointed at the ground.

"I didn't know . . ." Jazine mumbled.

"This here's private property, fucker! You got ten seconds to move your ass outa here!" The man grinned and raised his laser.

Judy had scrambled to her feet and reached for her bodysuit. "Just let us get dressed. We're terribly sorry . . ."

"Dressed, hell! Pick up your clothes and run! In five seconds we open up with our lasers!" The other guards chuckled, enjoying the sport.

Jazine and Judy grabbed up their suits and started running. Laughter followed them, and as they reached a gate a laser beam cut through a tree branch over their heads. There was more laughter, and then they were out.

150

They paused down the road to put on their suits. Catching her breath, Judy said, "Earl Jazine, that was the most terrible thing I've ever been through!"

"Don't complain. I got us out alive, didn't I?"

"But those men . . ."

"And luckily they didn't search our suits. If they'd found this printout from their computer, we would have been in big trouble!"

They reached the rocketcopter without further incident, and soon they were on their way back to New York. Once, in the night sky over the east coast, Judy glanced at him and blushed prettily.

In the morning Jazine put through an immediate check on the list of Nova's former employees. It took him only an hour, using tax returns, phone directories, and a few personal calls to establish that all were alive and well. The skeleton in the computer belonged to none of them.

He sat at his desk wondering about the next move, wondering especially how Carl Crader was managing his first meeting with Stanley Ambrose.

16.
EULER FROST

"It's decided, then?" Euler asked, speaking across the table to Graham Axman. "We attack the Utah installation?"

"It's decided." Axman frowned in annoyance. "I told you that at breakfast the other day."

"A great deal has happened since then," Euler pointed out. "Milly's murder, for one thing."

"A real tragedy."

Euler's eyes narrowed a bit, trying to read something into Axman's words. His first thought, on hearing of Milly's death, was to check on Axman's movements Monday night—but there was no proof that he'd left the farm. It was only a measure of Euler Frost's mind these days that he'd even entertained such a suspicion.

"I say we move immediately against the underground city," he told Axman. "Within the next twenty-four hours."

"So fast?"

"Milly is dead, and she was killed for a reason. I think she was killed by either Jason Blunt or Stanley Ambrose. It may mean Nova isn't going to wait for McCurdy's reelection next month before they try to take over the government."

Axman nodded. "I agree with that much, certainly. But we have fewer than twenty men. How do we go about attacking and destroying an underground computer center where hundreds of people live and work?"

In the days before his imprisonment, Graham Axman never would have asked such a question. Now, facing Euler across the table, he seemed to need some sort of reassurance from the younger man. The dream of the Fellowship of the HAND was still alive deep in his eyes, but it was a dream without a moving force.

"I have a plan," Euler said, unrolling a rubberized topographic map on the table. "The underground computer complex is in a former government missile defense base beneath this dry lake in Utah." He indicated a depression on the map's bumpy surface. "Obviously there must be air intakes and exhausts hidden here in addition to the entrance itself."

"But so well hidden that we'd never find them," Axman argued.

"We don't need to find them." Euler paused for a dramatic impact. "Suppose this dry lake became a real lake again. The water would get into the air intakes and flood the place. In the panic that followed, our job would be easy."

"But this is in the desert! How could you possibly fill it with water so quickly?"

"A cloudburst."

"A cloudburst? In the desert?"

"Where've you been, Graham? Haven't you ever heard of climate control and rain nights?"

"There's no climate control out there!"

"But there could be! The equipment is available in Denver—rocketcopters and cloud-seeding gear and cosmic generators. We could pour six inches of rain onto that area by this time tomorrow!"

"How? Steal the equipment? We don't know the first thing about its operation."

"But the government does, Graham. And the good old USAC is going to do our rain-making for us."

"Just like that?"

"Just like that. A vision-phone call from the Secretary of Climate Control in Washington."

"We kidnap him? Break into his office?"

"Nothing so crude. I have a video tape cassette of a speech he made to the International Conference on Climate Control last year. I've blocked out the audio and redubbed it with an electronic imitation of his voice. The face is the same, the mouth movements are the same—but now instead of calling upon the nations of the world to unite for worldwide weather control he's calling upon Denver to get out and make some rain over the Utah desert."

"It'll never work," Axman said, but there was interest in his eyes.

"It'll work. The secretary has a reputation as a stern, decisive man who takes no back-talk. He's been known to snap off his vision-phone during a conversation with congressmen. Out in Denver they'll see his face and hear his words exactly syncronized to the mouth movements. And they'll have no way of knowing they're seeing a taped replay rather than the man himself."

"What about background? You said it was at a

154

convention."

"The background is merely a gray wall. That's why I chose this particular cassette. Come into the other room and I'll run it for you."

He dropped the cassette into the slot and sat back to watch Axman's reaction. It was quite satisfactory. "That's a work of genius," the older man admitted. "The dubbing is perfect."

"It has to be, if our scheme is to work."

"The pause near the end. Is that rigged right? Will his answer fit their question?"

"I think so."

"And if they're suspicious?"

"It'll be after office hours in Washington. They won't be able to check. And why should they? What harm can a little rain in the desert do? I'm sure Denver knows nothing about the computers beneath that lake."

"If there's too much flooding, won't that harm our men too?"

Euler shook his head. "The rain will stop about the time we launch our attack. I've figured it very carefully."

Graham Axman sat back and smiled. "You've developed into a genius, Euler. What time do we call Denver?"

The call was placed at just after 6:00 P.M. Washington time, using a relay station to tie into the official capital circuits. Euler Frost was at the vision-phone, carefully adjusting the lens to aim it at the video set a few feet away. Axman was there too, and the black man, Sam Venray.

155

The circuits clicked and Euler saw the face of the Denver weather manager appear on the screen of the vision-phone. He flipped the switch and started playing the cassette.

"This is Secretary Baker in Washington," the image on the screen said.

"Yes, sir."

"How are things going out there?"

"Fine, sir. We . . ."

"Good. Look, we want to run a rain-making test over the Utah desert tonight. Think your rocket-copters can handle it?"

"That's sort of short notice, sir. If you could give us till . . ."

"Fine, fine! The area is bounded by map coordinates 78, 56, 79, 57. Latitude 38 degrees 50 minutes, longitude 113 degrees 10 minutes. Got that? 38-50, 113-10."

"I've got it. But . . ."

"We'd like about six inches to fall, at a rate of about a half inch an hour. Think you can do it? Whatever happens, stop all climate control operations by ten tomorrow morning. Got that?"

"Yes," the voice answered weakly.

"Any questions?"

"Could you tell me the reason for . . . ?"

"Good! Carry on, Williams."

"I'm not Williams. He's . . ."

"Goodnight."

The screen went blank, and the man in Denver sighed and switched off.

Frost and Axman sat there looking at each other, but it was Sam Venray who spoke first. "Hot damn!

156

Think he fell for it?"

"He fell for it," Euler answered enthusiastically. "Even that touch with the wrong name worked out well."

Axman was rubbing his hands together. "It's going to rain in Utah tonight!"

Euler Frost nodded and stood up. "Get the men together, Sam. We've got to be there in the morning."

The HAND rocketcopters encountered turbulence in the upper atmosphere while still a hundred miles from their destination. Rain was indeed falling over the entire area, and Euler only hoped that enough of it was draining into that dry lake. They swept over the area just after dawn, and he sighed with relief. The lake bottom was filling, and though the rain itself was beginning to let up, he knew the drainage would continue for several hours. The Denver people had done their job well.

"We're going in for a landing," he said to the pilot. "Tell the other copter."

Graham Axman peered over his shoulder, studying the gradually widening lake below. "How do we get into the place if the entrance is under water?"

"It won't be. They'll open it and come out before the water reaches it. And that's when we go in."

The twin rocketcopters settled onto the wet sand by the lake's edge. Euler Frost was the first one out, carrying his stunner and waving for the others to follow. Sam Venray hopped down from the second copter, a backpack of small but deadly hydrobombs bouncing as he ran. In the close confines below

157

ground, their concentrated destructive power would be most effective.

In that moment, with the eastern sun just breaking through the rain clouds to strike his face, Graham Axman looked a little like an avenging angel as he hefted a laser rifle and ran to join them. For just an instant Euler was sorry he'd won the battle and wondered if he really had.

He wondered if he dared turn his back on Graham Axman during the attack.

17.

CARL CRADER

He awakened to find Masha Blunt in his little cubicle, standing very close to the bed. Rubbing the sleep from his eyes and reaching for the contact pupils he wore, Crader was aware of a hum of activity that seemed foreign to the place.

"It's raining up above."

"Is that all?"

"Jason says it never rains here, at least not this much. It's a regular cloudburst and he's afraid it'll fill the lake bottom and flood us."

He rolled out of the narrow spring bed and stood up. "Strange. Sounds as if Climate Control may have bungled. Where's your husband?"

"Gone to greet Stanley Ambrose. You're to meet them in Jason's office."

He felt a hollow growling deep inside him. "What about breakfast?"

"They only serve capsule meals here. I guess that will have to do us."

"I suppose so," Crader grumbled, resigning himself to it."

He dressed quickly and met Masha at the little dining area. He was too old for things like capsule

159

meals, but he supposed he would survive a single day of it. As they headed down the corridor toward Blunt's office, he saw white-suited technicians operating a water pump along a wall where moisture was beginning to seep in. "That rain must really be heavy."

"I told you so! Jason is worried."

He had a sudden vision of a wall of water sweeping down upon them in some Biblical vengeance. Perhaps he should call Washington, notify Climate Control . . .

Suddenly Jason Blunt himself appeared ahead of them, crossing the corridor on the run. "Morning, Crader. Hope you slept well."

"Anything I can do?"

"Nothing. The rain seems to be stopping. We only have to hope it doesn't all drain into the lake. I'm having the entranceway opened as a safety measure, before the water reaches it and covers it over."

"I could call Washington if you need to evacuate."

"Washington is the last thing I need right now. It may have been Washington that caused it all in the first place!"

"What?"

"President McCurdy—remember? He's always hated my guts. And climate control can be a most effective political weapon."

"That's fantastic!"

"Is it? Then how else do you explain a cloudburst in the desert?"

"I don't know," Crader admitted, and he wondered if perhaps this was President McCurdy's way of striking out at Nova.

160

"Wait for me in the office," Blunt said, hurrying on. "I'll bring Ambrose in there as soon as we inspect the water damage to our computers."

Crader turned to Masha. "Then the mysterious Mr. Ambrose is really here."

"Oh yes."

They entered Jason Blunt's private office and Masha seated herself in one of the foamfold chairs. Crader moved behind the console to study the shelves of video cassettes and rarely seen books.

"Your husband is a reader, I see."

"Yes. He contends that all the world's knowledge cannot be found on video cassettes."

"He's right there." Crader let his eyes scan the shelf of books. Some were out-of-date, century-old titles like Ashby's *Design for a Brain,* Adler's *Thinking Machines,* Neville Moray's *Cybernetics,* and Norbert Wiener's *The Human Use of Human Beings.* Most were of a more recent vintage, though, and included Crankton's *Machines Our Masters,* Blacksmith's *Wonderland in Wires,* and Ongood's *Toward a Programmed Tomorrow.* There was even a copy of Lawrence Friday's book, *Animal Responsibilities in a Human Society,* the inventor's first attempt to relate the nervous system of animals to the computer sciences.

He took down the book by Wiener, to refresh his memory of twentieth-century views on computers, and noticed something odd about the back of the yellowed dust jacket. The author's picture had been defaced, scratched out and crossed over with a broad black marking pen. He was about to dismiss it as some century-old vandalism when he noticed that the

161

more recent books were the same way. On each of them, the author's picture had been defaced. He grunted and slipped the book back onto the shelf, wondering what it was about other men's faces that Jason Blunt hated so much.

"Do you read much?" Masha asked from across the room.

"Not a great deal, I'm sorry to say. With cassettes, one gets out of the habit of reading. And I suppose people your age don't read at all."

She shrugged. "The telenews printouts. That's about all. I sometimes wish I'd started reading books, but Stevro never wanted to bother with them."

"Speaking of Stevro, where is he this morning?"

"With Jason and Stanley Ambrose, I suppose. I haven't seen him."

Crader grunted and stooped to inspect the console, wishing again that Washington could afford something like this for his office. "A beautiful piece of equipment. It must have cost——"

His sentence was cut off by the silent sliding of the door, which opened to admit Jason Blunt and a slim, smiling man with an ashen face. "Hello again, Crader. I want you to meet the other half of Nova Industries—Stanley Ambrose."

"A pleasure."

Ambrose accepted his hand and bowed slightly. Close up, his face seemed drawn and unnaturally pale—the result, perhaps, of those years on Venus. "I have heard much of Carl Crader," he said. "The Computer Investigation Bureau has an enviable reputation."

162

"We try to live up to it."

"You'll forgive the confusion here this morning, but this rain was hardly to be expected."

"I understand."

Ambrose turned and bowed to Masha. "You have a charming wife, Jason."

"I think so."

He settled back into one of the white foamfold chairs, which only succeeded in making him appear even slimmer. "Now what was this business all of you had to discuss?"

Blunt held up a hand to Crader. "The government first."

"It's about this secret election which was held using the FRIDAY-404 election system. The President is most concerned that the system has been tarnished in such a manner, which you realize was against the law."

"Was it, now?" Stanley Ambrose allowed his smile to grow a bit wider. "As a former government employee myself, I was under the impression that such tax-financed facilities belonged to all the people. Since we did no harm to the election computers, I don't believe we violated any law."

"But what did you hope to accomplish?"

The slender man shrugged. "The computer was sitting there, not in use, and we had an election to be held. Since Nova employees and families number over eighty thousand and are scattered throughout the world, this seemed like the perfect way to conduct our election. It was my idea and I take full responsibility—or blame—for it."

"There are some reports that the entire Nova

163

operation is a plot to overthrow the government and substitute a computer-dominated society programmed to the past."

"Ridiculous!"

"I've been inspecting the wiring tunnels. The machines have learning and reasoning capabilities. They could easily be programmed to digest the facts and figures of our history and dictate the course of our future."

"To what purpose?"

Crader shrugged. "A preservation of the American dream? You tell me."

"There is no plot, Mr. Crader. We are a business like any other."

"Not quite like any other," Blunt interrupted.

Ambrose turned toward him. "What does that mean?"

"A year ago you came down from Venus and contacted me with your schemes. Of course Nova and this computer complex were already in existence, but when you bought into the business and we established a new corporation, things began to change. Learning capabilities were built into the computers. Sometimes I wonder myself what our real motives are. I wonder especially about this election we held for the new president of Nova."

"What about it?" Ambrose asked.

"The Nova employees include the employees of my oil drilling operation, and something very odd has been happening with them."

Crader sensed that this was a moment of confrontation between the two. He sat back and kept his mouth shut. Ambrose had gotten to his feet and was
164

facing Jason Blunt now. "I care nothing about your oil drilling."

"No? Then what about this?" Blunt pressed a button on his console and one of the doors along the far wall slid open. The bulky Stevro moved through the opening, looking like a wrestler in search of his opponent.

Stanely Ambrose blinked his pale eyes, as if trying to focus them on this sudden arrival. "I do not know this man," he said finally. "Should I know him?"

"His name is Stevro. He's from New Istanbul. Tell him what you told me, Stevro—about my drilling island in the Mediterranean."

"Well," Stevro began, "it happened like this. I run a sort of business in New Istanbul." He paused to glance over at Masha. "Sometimes I get to meet the drilling crews in the bars when they copter in for a weekend's rest."

Masha snorted. "You call that rest!"

"Anyway, I was talking to some of them, and this Nova election came up. They told me something about it—about you, Mr. Ambrose."

"I've never been to any drilling island."

"You didn't need to be. They've been diverting oil from the main pipeline, selling it to small companies in Greece and Italy. They told me you discovered it by means of the computer. You plotted the estimated yield against actual production, and ran a simulation on the computer to prove that the number of pump-hours reported on the generator record would have brought up more oil than the amount shipped."

"That makes me a very clever man if it's true," Ambrose remarked.

165

"There's more," Stevro said. "You used this information to blackmail them into voting as you ordered. You spoke to them by vision-phone and warned them you'd reveal their whole scheme if the votes from the Mediterranean weren't one hundred percent the way you ordered."

"Is it true?" Jason Blunt demanded. "Is it?"

Stanley Ambrose spread his hands in a gesture of surrender. "You have me at a disadvantage. Yes, it's true. Everything he says is true."

Stevro looked pleased. "Convinced?" he asked Blunt. "Now give me the money."

"But there's one thing," Ambrose said quietly. His right hand dipped into his pocket to extract an electric lighter. He kept them waiting while he lit a short cigar, and then he continued. "One thing. Did they tell you who I forced them to vote for?"

Stevro gave one of his jerky movements. "Yeah."

"Who?"

Head down, he mumbled, "Blunt."

"What?" Jason Blunt took a step forward, gripping the material of Stevro's bodysuit. "What is this? You didn't tell me this part before! You mean he blackmailed those men to vote *against* him in the election?"

"Well, yeah. That's the story I got. But that part seemed so fantastic I left it out."

They turned back to Stanley Ambrose, who was smiling just a bit smugly, in complete control of the situation. "Did you really think I'd try to fix the election in my favor, Jason?"

"Why did you do it?"

"I wanted you to win. I had enough responsibilities

166

on Venus. Now is simply a time for relaxing."

"But you *wanted* the election!"

"Yes."

"Why, if you didn't want to win?"

"Simply to have you elected in an official manner."

"I can't believe it," Jason Blunt said.

"It happened. It's the truth."

"You *forced* people to vote for me?"

Stanley Ambrose bowed slightly. "I tried to, in a few cases."

"Who won the election?"

"I did," Ambrose admitted. "But it was close. I came here today to show you the results, which you can verify in any way you wish."

"I can verify them," Crader said. "That's what started my involvement in this whole business—when a technician named Rogers stumbled upon the final figures in the FRIDAY-404 unit."

"Rogers? The one who was killed."

"The *first* one who was killed," Carl Crader reminded them. "Since then, a girl named Milly Norris has been murdered. And there's also the matter of the skeleton I discovered in the wiring tunnel here."

"Skeleton?" Ambrose's head jerked up. "What skeleton?"

Crader told him about the find in the sealed tunnel. "We think it might be an employee of your Lexington plant. My men are investigating that possibility now."

"Why Lexington?" Ambrose asked, truly puzzled.

"No one seems to be missing around here, and I found a shipping label from Lexington near the skeleton. I think the skeleton arrived here in a carton of computer parts and was hidden in the tunnel when it was sealed. A good place to hide a body, I suppose, in a dustproof, airtight tunnel that wasn't supposed to be opened for a generation."

"Not as good as the ground," Masha pointed out. "Why didn't they just bury the thing? Or throw it into a vacucinerator?"

"A good question," Crader admitted.

"The fact remains that a killer is loose." Jason Blunt moved in to take charge, as if this was his opportunity to best Ambrose. "If the killer is threatening Nova, then he's a threat to both Stanley and myself."

"Agreed," Ambrose said. "But I'm not convinced——"

He was interrupted by a loud buzzing from the console. "Emergency alarm," Blunt told them. "The water level may have reached the main entrance. If so, we'll have to evacuate."

He flipped on a closed-circuit video screen which showed the lake bed under water. But it was something beyond the water that glued their attention. Two rocketcopters stood at the edge of the lake, disgorging a score of armed men.

"My God!" Ambrose exclaimed. "Who are they? Government troops?"

Crader squinted at the screen. "Do you have a zoom lens?"

Blunt twisted a knob on the console and the running men jumped into sharp focus. Crader recognized Euler Frost and someone who could have been Graham Axman. "HAND," he said quietly.

168

"What?" shouted Blunt, halfway between a gasp and a scream.

"You're under attack by HAND. They want to blow up your computers."

"My God!" Stanley Ambrose's right hand shot beneath his jacket and came out holding a laser gun. "Are you all armed? We have to stop this!"

"Close the entrance," Crader ordered.

Blunt snapped two switches, and then a third. "I can't! The water has reached the controls!"

"We must have them outnumbered," Ambrose said, regaining his composure a bit but still keeping the laser in his hand. "We have two hundred men and women down here."

"But HAND is armed." Crader pointed to the screen. "That black man is carrying hydrobombs, just for a start."

"What'll we do?" Blunt asked.

In that moment, Crader ceased to think of them as revolutionaries. They were merely frightened businessmen who saw their major investment in jeopardy. "Get out there and hold them off! I'll contact Washington."

Blunt and Ambrose ran for help, with Stevro following, but Masha stayed at his side. "Will they kill us all?" she wanted to know.

"Not if we're lucky. They're after the machines."

He couldn't find an open circuit to the New White House, so he punched up New York, hoping that Earl was in the office early this morning. The vision-phone screen crackled and swam, finally settling down to show Judy at her desk.

"Judy, is Earl in? Emergency!"

"He's here. Wait till you hear what happened down in Lexington!"

"No time now, Judy. Switch me."

"Right."

Earl Jazine came on the screen. "I just finished checking out those former Nova employ——"

"We're under attack, Earl. HAND is attacking the Utah complex. Get help here!"

The screen went blank, and Crader didn't know if Earl had hung up or some relay point had been cut. He only hoped the message had gotten through.

"Come on," he told Masha.

"Where?"

A dull, booming thud reached them, shaking the room and bringing terror to her eyes. Before she could speak, he said, "That was a hydrobomb. They must be inside. Is there a back way out of here?"

Jason Blunt appeared at the door, his eyes terror-stricken. "They're blowing up the place!"

"Are they inside?"

"A few of them. We're fighting them at the entrance, and they haven't gotten down the elevators yet."

"I'd suggest getting your wife out of here. Is there an emergency exit of some sort?"

"There is one," he confirmed, "but it only leads up to the desert. She wouldn't be safe there with these HAND people prowling around. I could get you down to the far end of our complex, though, near that exit. If HAND breaks through, you'd be close enough to escape."

"Good. I called for help before the vision-phones went out, but I don't know if my message got

170

through."

Blunt ran to the console and confirmed that outside communications were cut off. "I'll have somebody guide you," he said. "As you know, Crader, it's very easy to get lost down here." He spoke over an intercom system to some unseen person. "Vikor, I'm sending some people down to you. Take them to zone seven and wait there with them."

At that moment Stevro reappeared from somewhere, his chest heaving with the strain of some unaccustomed exertion. "They've got lasers and stunners! And bombs! They want to kill us all!"

"No," Crader said. "Not us—only the machines."

Blunt saw at once that the big Turk would contribute little to their defense. "You'd better go with Masha and Crader," he said. "Out that door and down the passage to the end. Vikor will be waiting there to take you the rest of the way. Zone seven should be safe, since it's beyond the machine areas, back in the living quarters. They won't bother to come that far. And if they do, Vikor will show you the escape hatch. Trust him. He's a good man—one of our best technicians."

A series of dull thuds reached them, like the concussions of distant bombs. "Let's go," Crader ordered.

Jason Blunt put a hand on his arm. "One thing—you know some of those people. Could you talk to them? Stop them?"

Crader shook his head. "I've called for help. That's all I can do." He knew that Frost and Axman would not be turned aside now.

"All right. I just think of all this equipment, all my

computers . . ." He sighed at the thought. "Go now, down this corridor to the end. Vikor is waiting."

His office door slid shut behind them, and Crader led the way quickly down a long passageway lit by a radiant stripe along the ceiling. Behind them there were more dull thuds, not as loud as the first hydro-bomb had been. "What are those?" Masha asked.

"Both sides are using stunners. In a confined space, the concussion from a stunner makes a noise like that. That's the least of our worries. When it gets too quiet it may mean they're using laser guns."

"They'll kill my husband," Masha said without emotion, making it a simple statement of fact.

"He may be lucky. They just want the machines."

Panting to keep up with them, Stevro said, "If he dies you can come back with me, Masha dear."

"What? To be sold again?" Her anger flared briefly.

"No, no. I am out of that business."

"Sure! Now you only try to shake down millionaires like Jason with your sad bits of information."

"I thought I was doing him a favor."

"By telling him only part of the truth? By turning him against Stanley Ambrose?"

Crader could see the end of the corridor, where it intersected another, wider passageway. A man waited there in the shadows for them, his right profile showing smooth, nondescript features.

"Are you Vikor?"

"Yes. Come this way. Quickly!"

He led them to the right, down the wider passageway, to an area Crader had missed on his first visit.

There were sleeping quarters for the technicians, and even small apartments for those who lived here with their families. In some rooms as they passed he could see the artificial sunlight bathing the sparse furnishings in a sort of golden glow.

A woman came out of one of the rooms and asked, "Are we in danger?"

"No," Vikor told her. "Go back inside and slide the door shut."

"How many are there here?" Crader asked.

Walking slightly ahead and to his left, Vikor merely grunted. He did not seem willing to give out any unnecessary information.

Presently they reached a widening in the passage, apparently designed as an underground recreation area. There was plastic grass in an odd shade of emerald green, and picnic tables clustered around a little stream. Artificial sunlight made it almost as bright as outdoors.

"Sit down," Vikor instructed them, motioning toward the tables. "We will wait here."

"The exit is nearby?" Crader asked.

Vikor nodded. "Nearby." He gestured toward a spiral stairway.

"Will we be safe here?" Masha asked.

"You will be safe as long as you stay with me," Vikor said. "I will take care of you."

He turned to face Masha as he spoke, and for the first time Crader saw the odd tattooed design on his left cheek.

18.
GRAHAM AXMAN

At the beginning the attack went well.

Running along behind Euler Frost, carrying his laser rifle, Axman felt the old surge that impending combat always brought him. He had decided back on the farm that there was no point in opposing Frost openly for control of HAND. It was better to go along with him and attack the Nova complex. Anything could happen then. In the midst of the battle, Frost might even be killed or captured—and then the problem would no longer exist.

The months in prison had changed Axman, as he would have been the first to admit. They had radicalized him, but in a particular way. No longer was he content to smash out at those institutions that would use the machines as a substitute for free will. Now he wanted to smash all institutions, beginning with the government which had imprisoned him.

But there was time.

First, the attack on Nova. Then, later, when he was fully in command again, he could turn his attention to the New White House.

Right now, as the entrance to the underground city loomed up before them, his thoughts were on the battle of the moment. He could see that the level of the lake water had reached the lowest of the air intakes, which meant there would be some flooding below. And the open entrance was awash with shallow splashing as Euler Frost ran to it. Though the rain itself had stopped, water continued to empty into the lake bed.

"Get that one!" he shouted suddenly to Frost as a head popped up in the opening. Frost fired a quick blast of his stunner and the man toppled back inside. Then they had gained the entrance, jamming the door so it couldn't be closed.

Frost glanced around, like a general surveying the battleground. "Sam!" he called to Venray. "Get ready with your hydrobombs. Graham—use the laser rifle on that communications relay!"

Axman nodded and sighted along the rifle. It was no more effective, really, than a laser pistol, but its wider beam made cutting jobs go quicker. He squeezed the trigger and watched the beam shoot out to the distant hilltop, slicing through the supports of the relay tower. As the tower toppled over on its side, he released the trigger and followed the others inside. At least no one down below would be using a vision-phone or radio relay.

Below ground they had forced open the doors of the elevator shaft and Venray dropped a hydrobomb inside. There was a thudding boom that seemed to shake the entire earth, filling the upper level with smoke and dust.

"Masks on," Euler Frost ordered. "We may have to use smoke bombs."

It was the Federal Medical Center all over again,

only this time he wouldn't be captured. This time it would be Euler Frost who took the fall.

There was a series of dull thuds ahead as someone opened fire with a stunner. Frost had found the stairs by the elevator and started down. Sam Venray glanced over at Axman and said, "Stay close. We'll need that laser."

"I'm right behind you."

Below, when they reached the main level, the sight was staggering. Huge rooms, their walls covered with computers and teleprinters and information retrieval systems. Wires and lights and telescreens. The very latest in cathoid ray equipment. And all bathed in constant light from radiant ceilings.

"I'm impressed," Axman shouted to Frost over the thud of the stunners.

"Get to work with the laser. Sam, plant your hydrobombs."

But it was not to be quite that easy. Ahead, counterattacking through the smoke and haze, came a score of armed technicians. Some carried stunners, and at least one had an old-fashioned bullet-firing revolver. There was a single shot from it and the man on Axman's right screamed and toppled backwards, grabbing at his chest.

Sam Venray cursed and went down on one knee, hurling a hydrobomb like a hand grenade at the nearest machine. There was a fiery blast as the bomb went off, then a shower of sparks from the electrical fire.

"Smoke bombs!" Frost shouted, seeing another of his men topple before the counterattack.

In the instant before the smoke closed in, Axman
176

aimed his laser rifle and cut through the stomach of the man with the revolver.

"Don't kill unless necessary," Frost yelled at him and turned away.

"That was necessary."

He shifted the laser ever so slightly, targeting Euler Frost's back in the sights. Then the smoke closed in and he lost him.

"This way," Sam Venray said after a moment, reaching out to guide him, and Axman wondered if the black man had X-ray eyes that penetrated the smoke. Then he realized that some of the HAND people were wearing night-goggles, and he wished he'd brought a pair himself.

Venray finished attaching hydrobombs to each of the computer banks and then pulled Axman along down a corridor that led deeper into the underground city. Frost already stood before a locked metal door marked EXECUTIVE OFFICES.

"Use the laser," he ordered Axman. "I think they're inside."

The beam cut quickly through the metal, circling the locking mechanism until it fell away. Then Axman used the barrel of the rifle to slide the door open.

It was a massive office, with white foam chairs and a large desk console at one end. There were two men inside, both holding laser pistols. When Axman saw them, he started to swing his own rifle around, but the man with the short black beard fired first, slicing the barrel of his weapon.

"Those rifles make an easy target," he said calmly. "Stand where you are."

Euler Frost stepped forward. "You must be Jason Blunt. We meet at last."

"Frost?"

"Yes." He turned to the other, a slim, pale man, and said, "Stanley Ambrose, I presume. We never had the pleasure of meeting during my stay on Venus."

Ambrose bowed slightly, his grip steady on the laser pistol in his right fist. "You presume correctly. And this is my first meeting with the forces of HAND."

"And your last," Euler Frost said. "We'll give you an opportunity to clear everyone out of here before we blow it all up."

"But we seem to have the lasers," Ambrose pointed out, gesturing to include Jason Blunt at his side.

"My men have wired hydrobombs to all your machines. If you kill us they'll be detonated by radio waves and this whole place will go up—or down, as the case may be." He let his eyes travel to the radiant ceiling.

"The city was built to withstand bombing," Jason Blunt said. "You forget it was originally a missile defense command post. And hydrobombs are only effective within a concentrated area of a few feet."

"Shall we test it, then, against the force of twenty hydrobombs?" Euler Frost's voice was filled with confidence.

For a moment Axman thought it would be a standoff. But then one of the HAND men ran in, splashing through the shallow water that was beginning to collect in the corridor. "Army rocketcopters landing above!" he shouted. "Should I blast the computers?"

178

Jason Blunt turned and drilled him through the middle with a laser beam. In the same instant, Sam Venray dropped to his knees and flipped the half-empty backpack of hydrobombs directly at Blunt and Ambrose.

Frost moved in and Axman followed, using his damaged rifle as a club. Ambrose turned and ran as the hydrobombs scattered across the floor. Blunt, unnerved and uncertain, tried to bring his pistol around for another shot but Axman hit him across the temple with the rifle butt.

"Are those timed?" Frost yelled to the black man.

"Not yet," Venray grinned, scooping up the fallen hydrobombs. "But it sure worried them!"

"I'll go after Ambrose," Axman said, but as he reached the corridor he realized the hopelessness of the task. The pale man had already disappeared into the smoke.

He turned back into the room and saw that Blunt was on the floor, dazed by the blow, with blood from a scalp cut speckling the shaggy white rug.

"There must be another way out of here," Euler Frost reasoned. "Blow the machines, Sam, and we'll take our chances. Another five minutes and it'll be too late."

The sound of the stunners reached them, and Venray called from the doorway. "It's already too late. The Nova technicians are counterattacking, dismantling the bombs!"

"Do what you can!" Frost ordered. Then, to Axman, he said, "Come on!"

"What about Blunt?"

"Leave him."

"It'll be safer to kill him now."

"Leave him, I said!" Euler Frost barked. "I told you we don't kill unless necessary."

He bent to scoop up Blunt's fallen laser pistol and then ran into the corridor with Axman following.

As they watched, one of Venray's hydrobombs exploded in a burst of liquid fire, tearing the front from a million-dollar computer and leaving it a mass of mangled wreckage and crackling, arcing wires. The force of the explosion knocked loose panels from the radiant ceiling, which were dropping among the dead and wounded in the smoke-filled chamber.

"Troops coming down the stairs," Venray warned. Two more computer banks exploded, but then he cursed and said, "I can't set off the others! The short circuits are interfering with my radio waves."

"This way, then," Frost decided. "Ambrose ran down here somewhere. There may be a way out."

They fought their way through the smoke, splashing through occasional puddles of water. Axman had picked up a fallen stunner, discarding the ruined laser rifle, and he held it ready as he ran. Once, when a white-suited technician lunged at them from a cross-passage, he downed the man with a close-range blast.

"We'll be lost in here," Axman said as they ran on. The smoke was clearing now, but there seemed nothing ahead but more passageways and rooms.

They passed another row of smaller computers, built into the rocky walls of the corridor. Venray paused long enough to attach hydrobombs to two of them, with a wire strung across the passage about a foot off the floor. "If they come following us, they'll get a surprise," he said with a chuckle.

They started to move off, but suddenly Frost hesitated. "No," he decided, "unhook it, Sam. There are still HAND people back there. We might kill our own men."

Sam shrugged and did as he was told. As he bent to his task, Axman went to help, and carefully slipped one of the hydrobombs into his own pocket. It could come in handy later, and it was much more effective than the stunner he carried.

They hurried on along the passage, past separate cubicles that were obviously living quarters. "Zone seven," Frost said, reading a wall sign. "On the chart in Blunt's office, zone seven was the outer one, at the very back of the complex. There was some indication of an exit here."

"I sure hope so!" Venray said. Behind them, far in the distance, the thud of stunners echoed.

"Somebody up ahead," Axman cautioned. They were coming to a widening in the passage, a recreation area with artificial grass underfoot. He could see a group of people half hidden by the picnic tables and chairs of the underground park. There were three—two men and a woman.

"Hold up," Frost said. "I recognize one of them. It's Carl Crader!"

"So it is," Axman agreed. His hand closed around the hydrobomb in his pocket. To kill Crader might be a real bonus, even more than killing Euler Frost.

Then suddenly there was another voice behind them. "Walk slowly, hands up, or you're dead!"

Axman turned just far enough to glimpse a man with an odd tattooed design on his left cheek. He was covering them all with two laser pistols.

19.

MASHA BLUNT

She had never been so terrified in her life.

The waiting in the silent, man-made park under the earth, with the rays of some artificial sun beating down upon them, had been bad enough. But now suddenly the threat of violence emerged again. The man with the tattooed face had heard someone approaching and had hidden himself in a service closet along the passageway. When the three men passed, he stepped out, covering them with laser pistols.

"They're the leadership of HAND," Carl Crader said, hurrying forward. "Euler Frost and Axman. I don't know the black man."

At Masha's side, Stevro grunted and spoke in a low voice. "This might be our chance to get away, my dear, if you want to go. There's a spiral stairway over there, leading up through a metal shaftway. That man Vikor said it was the way out."

But she didn't know what she wanted. Watching Vikor disarm the three from HAND, she thought for a moment that the worst was over, that they might still all make it out of this place alive.

But then, with a sudden movement almost too quick to follow, the man Crader identified as Axman leaped forward, grabbing Euler Frost as a shield.

"All right, Crader!" he shouted. "This is a hydrobomb. Call off your man or we all die."

"Don't be a fool," Frost said, struggling to free himself from Axman's grip.

Carl Crader was walking forward, ignoring Axman's threat. "You wouldn't use Euler for a shield, Graham. HAND needs him too badly." He motioned Vikor away, but the tattooed man still held his lasers.

"HAND doesn't need him at all! Go on and kill him—it'll save me the trouble later!"

"Give me that hydrobomb, Graham," Crader said, reaching out his hand.

Graham Axman snarled and pushed Frost forward into Crader. He stepped back and was raising his arm to hurl the hydrobomb when suddenly it exploded with an ear-splitting roar, drenching Axman in a sea of liquid fire.

Within seconds there was nothing left of him but a heap of flames, burning brightly against the emerald green of the artificial grass.

The blast of the hydrobomb had knocked Masha down, but she struggled to her feet and hurried to help the others. No one seemed badly hurt, although Crader and Frost, closest to the explosion, were bruised and shaken as they stood up.

"I don't know how it happened," Crader said, inspecting a minor blast burn on his hand, "but I'm certainly thankful it did."

Euler Frost glanced over at the black man. "Sam?" he questioned.

183

Venray nodded and produced a tiny transistorized device from his pocket. "I set it off with a radio wave. Hated to do it to Graham, but it was him or us. He was really crazy."

"Yes," Frost said, staring down at the burning heap. To Masha he looked as if he'd lost an old friend.

"I can still hear stunners," Crader said.

Frost turned to him. "Your people again. The troops to the rescue."

"Where's my husband?" Masha blurted out. "Have you killed him?"

"He was alive the last we knew. Just a bump on the head."

Venray looked uncertainly at Vikor, who still held his laser guns. Then he said to Frost, "We'd better keep moving."

Frost nodded. "We're going out the other exit, Crader."

But the CIB director shook his head. "I let you escape once before, Euler, after the attack on the medical center. This time you stay. Perhaps you can convince a court of law that your cause is just."

"Axman didn't convince anyone."

"Axman didn't try."

Frost turned to the black man. "Go on, Sam. I'll stay here."

"You'll both stay," Crader said. "There's a great deal to be explained here, and until it is, no one is leaving."

There were shouts from along the passage, and the sound of others approaching. Masha wondered who it would be this time—more of HAND, or the army

184

troops, or maybe even her husband and Ambrose? Whoever it was, she wanted to get away from here, wanted to go back to the island, where life was so much simpler.

She saw Jason first, leading the way, and after that she saw no one else. Her vision blurred with tears and for the first time in her life she realized that she really loved the man for all his faults. What had started as mere sexual attraction back in New Istanbul had grown into something much more.

Now, seeing the spots of blood along his temple, she wanted to run to him. But before she could move, Crader called out, "Earl! Over here, Earl!"

He was calling to a younger member of the party, a handsome man who wore smoke goggles and carried a stunner. But even as she saw him, backed by a dozen battle-ready troops, she felt a sudden yank on her arm that spun her around, off balance.

"That's him," the man named Earl shouted. "The one with the tattoo! He tried to kill me at the zooitorium!"

But the man named Vikor already had his laser to her forehead, pulling her along in some mad embrace as he ran toward the stairs going up. "Don't struggle," he rasped in her ear. "Don't struggle. I have killed many like you."

Crader and Earl started after them, but Vikor sent them scattering with a blast from his laser. It was Jason, running hard, who came closest, and he barked a quick command. "Vikor—let her go! Are you mad?"

But then Crader had her husband by the arm, pulling him back. "He doesn't obey you, Blunt. He never has."

185

"But that's Vikor! He works for me."

"Not you, Blunt. He works for Stanley Ambrose, and he's a murderer. I spotted him at once from Earl's description, but I wanted to see if he might lead us to Ambrose."

"But . . ."

"Careful! He's already killed a man named Rogers, and probably Milly Norris as well. And a third person too."

Vikor pulled her along, now at the base of the spiral stairs, and forced her to climb ahead of him into the darkness. With the laser he held off pursuit and started up after her. "No tricks," he said. "Or, I'll kill you."

"Where are you taking me?"

"Out of here. Away." He nudged her in the small of the back with his pistol. "Keep climbing!"

"These stairs go on forever. We must be a hundred feet below ground!"

But he forced her on, prodding her with the weapon. She was all but exhausted from the climb when she heard a light scraping of metal from above.

Someone was ahead of them on the stairs!

She held her breath, then coughed, hoping the sound would cover the footfalls from above. "What is it?" Vikor demanded.

"Nothing. I . . . I have to stop. I'm out of breath."

"Keep climbing!"

She peered into the darkness above, trying to make out a human form. Had it only been a rat or some desert creature she'd heard?

Then suddenly there was someone really there, pressing past her to grapple with Vikor. She recog-
186

nized the familiar harsh odor of soilweed and knew that it was Stevro.

Stevro, good old Stevro.

Escaping himself, but taking time to rescue her. She hadn't even realized he was missing after he'd asked her to come along, but obviously he'd used the hydrobomb explosion to cover his exit.

"Stevro!" she gasped. "I can't see you!"

"That's all right, my dear," he gasped, very close to her. "I got you into this, back in the beginning. I guess it's up to me to get you out."

They were struggling for the laser pistol on the narrow spiral stairway, and she could see neither of them in the darkness.

Then there was a gasp from Vikor and the weapon clattered down the steps. Stevro moved in for the kill, and it was only too late that she remembered the tattooed man's second gun.

Stevro, he has another!

"Stevro, he has another!"

But the laser beam jumped and cut, lighting the darkness for an instant. She saw Stevro take it full in the stomach and start to fall.

In that instant, when he must have felt death very close, Stevro still managed to hang on, to fling himself at his murderer. There was a gasping scream torn from Vikor's throat, and then both of them toppled over the railing down fifty feet to the bottom.

For a long time Masha clung there sobbing, frozen in position. They had to come and get her, coaxing her gently down.

But then there was Jason to comfort her, and Carl Crader to say, "Come now. Come, come. It'll be all right. It's almost over now."

187

20.
CARL CRADER

Earl Jazine came up shaking his head. "There was no one missing from that Lexington plant, chief. I checked them all out. But there's someone missing right here. The troops have searched the entire city, every room in the place, and there's no sign of Stanley Ambrose. He must have escaped up through that emergency exit before you reached it."

The medic had treated Crader's scorched hand, and crews were busy cleaning up the damage done by the flooding and HAND's assault. The bodies of Graham Axman and Stevro and Vikor had been removed along with the other casualties. In the executive office, Jason Blunt sat with his wife, waiting for the final scene of the drama. Near them, handcuffed together, sat Euler Frost and Sam Venray.

"He didn't escape," Crader said. "Stevro came back down those stairs because he couldn't get the exit open. The rain short-circuited the electric release latch. No one went out of there today."

Jazine scratched his head. "But he couldn't have gone back the other way to the main entrance. The troops were coming in, and they rounded everybody up till they could sort them out. I got here just a little after that, and I can tell you nobody left."

"I believe you, Earl." Crader sat down in one of the foamfold chairs, letting his eyes wander over the splotches of blood and water and dirt on the white shag rug. Somehow it seemed a reflection of all that was Nova Industries at the moment.

"Then what happened to him?"

Carl Crader thought about it. He thought about Nova and Jason Blunt and the Venus Colony and HAND, and everything that had happened during the past weeks. Mostly he thought about Andrew Jackson McCurdy and what it must be like to be president of the United States and Canada.

Finally he roused himself and said to Jazine, "Come on. We're going to get him."

"You know where he is?"

"I know the only place he could possibly be."

He took a laser pistol from one of the army officers, though he hated using a weapon to kill. With Jazine at his side he led the way across the main computer area, still wet and smoky from the siege. Jason Blunt had trailed along behind them, and Crader asked, "How bad is the damage?"

"Nearly half our computers were destroyed," Blunt said sadly. "And a good deal of the taped records. It finishes us for a long time to come."

Crader nodded silently.

"Where are you taking us?" Jazine asked as they rounded a corner.

Crader stopped before the familiar door with its broken seals. "These are the wiring tunnels where I found the skeleton. The troops wouldn't have thought to look here."

"You think he's inside?"

"I know he is. It's the only place."

Crader slid the door open and stepped into the tunnel once more. The light was even dimmer now, because many of the computer banks had been knocked out in the siege. The glow from their transitubes came through only at irregular intervals.

Shining his wrist-light before him, Crader moved deeper into the tunnel. "Ambrose? Stanley Ambrose? Are you here?"

At first there was no response, but after he called out twice more they heard a far-off reply. Presently, following the voice to its source, they found Stanley Ambrose huddled against one of the glowing circuit panels.

"Are you all right?" Blunt asked, helping the man to his feet.

"I . . . I think so. Is it over?"

"It's over for you," Crader said. "I'm placing you under arrest."

Ambrose shook off Jason Blunt's helping hand. "Arrest? On what charge, may I ask? We were the ones attacked by those outlaws from HAND, remember."

And Blunt joined in. "Is this still part of your wild idea about a plot to overthrow the government, Crader?"

"The plot was a long-range one, very complex. It was not an overthrow of the government at all. Quite the contrary, as a matter of fact."

"Then why are you arresting me?" Ambrose asked again.

"For murder. Vikor is dead, and I imagine he did

190

the actual killings, but only on your orders. There are three that I know about, plus the attempt on Earl Jazine here."

"Three?"

Crader nodded. "A computer engineer named Harry Rogers, a woman named Milly Norris, and of course the real Stanley Ambrose."

"What?" It was a gasp from Blunt. "But this is Ambrose!"

"No, no." Crader shook his head and took a firm grip on his prisoner. "I think when we remove all the makeup we'll find someone quite different underneath. I think we'll find the inventor of the election computer—Professor Lawrence Friday."

Later, when they'd gathered back in Jason Blunt's office, and Lawrence Friday had been taken away, Crader explained. "You see, he never wanted to overthrow the government—he simply wanted to be president of the USAC himself. And that was his problem. Because, of course, the single person in this country who could never be elected president of the FRIDAY-404 computer was the man who invented it. Public opinion would never allow such a thing. There'd always be those who would claim he knew how to cheat the machine."

"And he did," Jazine said.

Crader nodded. "Yes, he did. Later I hope he'll tell us exactly how it was done, but I imagine his system consisted of supplying an extra electrical impulse. In simple terms, if candidate A is computerized by a dash, or a long electrical impulse, and candidate B by a dot or short impulse, it's not too

191

difficult to imagine adding impulses to B's signal to make it look like A's."

"So he could fix the election," Blunt agreed. "What does that have to do with killing Stanley Ambrose and taking his place?"

"Well, if Friday couldn't run for president under his own identity, then he needed to assume another one, right? But whose identity, and how? Obviously, a candidate for president has to be someone in the public eye, preferably already in the government. But for Friday's purpose it also had to be someone completely cut off from family and friends—someone who could be successfully impersonated without the ruse being discovered. And who fit those qualifications perfectly?"

"Stanley Ambrose."

"Correct—Stanley Ambrose. A man without a family, a man who had just spent five years as director of the Venus Colony. He was a member of government, well known to the public, and yet he had been quite literally *on another planet for the past five years!* Anyone can change a great deal in five years. Even new quirks of personality could be put down to the hardships of life on Venus."

"When did he kill the real Ambrose?" Blunt wanted to know.

"As soon as he returned from Venus, a year ago. Then, of course, Friday—Ambrose had to go into hiding—for two reasons. First, to protect his new Ambrose identity from too many prying newsmen, and second, to continue his existence as Lawrence Friday. I said this was a long-range scheme, and its target date was still four years away. Sometime in those four years, Friday would 'die' and Stanley Ambrose would come out of seclusion to begin his campaign for the presidency."

"How did he know he'd get the nomination?" Blunt asked.

"The primary elections could be fixed the same as the national election. And since primary results are binding on the party, there would have been no way to stop him."

"Let's get back to this dying," Earl said. "How would he work that?"

"I doubt if he knew all the details himself yet. But I do know he kept a skeleton—probably Stanley Ambrose's skeleton—in reserve in case it was needed. That's why the skeleton was sealed away in that tunnel instead of being buried. I imagine he lured the real Ambrose to the Lexington plant last year on some pretext or other, killed him or had Vikor do it, dissolved the flesh with acid or ultrasonic waves, and shipped the skeleton out here to Utah. Sometime during the next four years, if necessary, it could become the skeleton of Lawrence Friday."

"That's horrible," Masha said. She was sitting very close to her husband, and it was the first time she'd spoken.

"Horrible, yes. But necessary to his plan. You see, once he was really in the public eye, with all his time accounted for, leading a double life would be impossible. He would become Stanley Ambrose, late of the Venus Colony, now a candidate for president. He would win the nomination, he would win the election. And only then, four years from now, would he make use of this massive computerized history by Nova In-

193

dustries. Only then would the machines take over, with a little human help from him, of course."

"But how did you know all this?" Blunt asked.

"There were many things—call them clues if you will. First, there was the doubt about the identity of Stanley Ambrose. Last week, Earl, you showed me copies of some photographs of Ambrose taken by Milly Norris at a picnic before he went to Venus. They showed him pitching softball with his left hand. And yet the man I met here today lit a cigar with his right hand, and held a laser pistol with his right hand. That at least gave me reason to doubt that he was the real Stanley Ambrose. Then too, there was the murder of Milly Norris. Why was she killed? When I considered that question in light of the possibility that Ambrose might be a fake, the answer was immediately obvious. Ambrose was a man without family or close friends. Only Milly Norris, his mistress of six years ago, would be likely to realize the truth. I think Friday went to her the other night in his Ambrose disguise to see if he could fool her. It was to be the supreme test, and I imagine Vikor was standing close by with his laser gun. Of course we know what happened. Friday—Ambrose failed the test. Perhaps she saw through his disguise. Or perhaps he lit a cigar with his right hand and she remembered he was left-handed. In any event, she had to die."

Earl Jazine merely shook his head. "But even if you suspected it was a fake Ambrose, how in hell did you know the man behind the fake was Lawrence Friday?"

"Several things told me that, Earl. For one, Vikor

first tried to kill you after you'd questioned Friday about the election computer. And Vikor killed Rogers and erased the election results after you told Friday of your findings."

"But Friday was the one who first suggested a secret election."

"Of course. But only because he'd already signaled Vikor to kill you when you left him, and ordered him to kill Rogers as well. Both Friday and Ambrose were about the same size, general appearance, and age, which is probably one reason Friday chose Ambrose to impersonate—that and the fact he'd been on Venus for five years. Two things really tipped me off, though. The day we took Friday to Washington to confer with President McCurdy, he knew that the results of the private election had been fed into a computer in Chicago. Yet none of us had told him. Moreover, while I was waiting to meet him today, I discovered that someone had disfigured the faces of the authors on the jackets of all those books behind your console, Blunt."

"What?"

Crader nodded. "At first I thought you'd done it yourself. But then the true explanation became obvious to me. One jacket had a photograph of Lawrence Friday on it. Few people would be admitted to this private office, but certainly your partner Stanley Ambrose had been one of them. On one visit Friday disfigured those pictures so you wouldn't be struck by anything familiar in the portrait of himself—a glint of the eyes, perhaps, or a tilt of the head. With your youthful video experience, he knew you must have a knowledge of the makeup skills available to

195

actors today—face foam and voice boxes and the like. He couldn't gamble on your seeing his picture without makeup and making the connection in your mind. Of course stealing or disfiguring that one book would merely have called attention to it, so he obliterated all the authors' photos."

"My God!" Jason Blunt merely stared at the shelf of books. "The man is mad!"

"But a mad genius. Knowing Ambrose wasn't real, and that Friday was masquerading as him, I still had to ask myself why. The election computer was the only tie-in between the men, and then I realized his scheme. I should have tumbled to it much sooner, of course, because consider this—why should Nova Industries, with the largest computer complex in the nation, with vision-phone communications to all its employees throughout the world, go to the risk of tying their secret election into the FRIDAY-404 system? The answer now is obvious. This whole secret election was just Friday's excuse to test the system, to see if it could be fixed in the way he thought possible. To be certain he could change specific votes, he even blackmailed the men of the Mediterranean drilling island into voting for you, Blunt. Then he changed their votes to his side. He won the secret election, but only as a test for the bigger one to come in four years."

"A fantastic scheme!"

"It was that," Crader agreed. "But perhaps without HAND to force the issue, it could have succeeded."

"What'll happen to the HAND people you captured?"

"They'll be tried, of course. But I'd like to see their trial go into the broader issues of this whole affair. Despite everything you've told me, Blunt, you were setting up a computer city here. You and the fake Ambrose had designs on this country of ours, and I don't think they were designs for the best. We can never be ruled by the past, no matter how pleasant and agreeable that past has been. You can't freeze time, and you can't program progress in terms of the past."

Jason Blunt didn't answer. He helped Masha to her feet and they walked out, past the rows of damaged computers. Crader had the distinct impression that he was already planning for some sort of tomorrow.

The rocketcopter landed on the World Trade Center just at sundown, and Crader and Jazine went downstairs to the office where Judy was waiting for them.

"I thought you'd be gone by now, Judy," Crader said, lifting the cartridge from his pocket transcribing unit.

"I stayed in case you wanted me to get the report off to President McCurdy tonight."

"We finished it on the copter coming in. Put it on the autotype and send it down by phone-vision copier in the morning."

He tossed her the cartridge and she caught it with one hand. "Did Earl tell you what he did to me down in Lexington?"

"He saved your life, from the way I hear it."

"I don't think I could stand having my life saved

that way every day."

Crader smiled and turned to Earl. "Think you could get into that Lexington plant again—without Judy and through the front door this time?"

"I guess so, chief."

"Try it tomorrow. Vikor is dead, and we've got Friday, but there may have been others involved. Check their visitors' register for the date of Ambrose's first visit. We need to establish as closely as possible just when he was killed."

"I'll take care of it, chief."

Crader nodded. From the outer office he could hear Judy starting up the autotype. Nobody seemed ready to go home yet. He glanced out the window at the sun setting over the Jersey meadows, then sighed and swung back to his desk to read the day's reports.